HEALING RAIN

The Rain King

F. L. Raynaud

Book One – Sons of Thunder Series

Dream Weaver Publication
ANNA MARIA, FLORIDA

F. L. Raynaud/Dream Weaver Publication
P.O. Box 503
Anna Maria, FL, 34216

www.DreamWeaver.org www.SeersGift.com

Publisher's Note: This is a work of fiction. Names, characters, places, and incidents are a product of the author's imagination. Locales and public names are sometimes used for atmospheric purposes. Any resemblance to actual people, living or dead, or to businesses, companies, events, institutions, or locales is completely coincidental.

Cover Art ©iStock.com/Anže Mulec
Cover Design ©2014 Dream Weaver Publishing
Book Layout ©2013 BookDesignTemplates.com

Ordering Information:
Quantity sales. Special discounts are available on quantity purchases by corporations, associations, and others. For details, contact the "Special Sales Department" at the address above.

Sons of Thunder Series, Book One: Healing Rain - The Rain King / F. L. Raynaud. -- 1st ed.
ISBN 978-0-9905959-4-6

In Memoriam

Myrtle Jean Raynaud, Robert Lancing Lucas, Liberty Earnest Raynaud, and Jamisen Liberty Raynaud

To

Buddie Paul Raynaud
This book is my prayer for you...

To all who suffer from terminal illness and cancer Let it Rain...

Acknowledgement

I would like to thank everyone who encouraged me to write. I want to thank my dear friend Ashley Shepherd for her amazing words of encouragement and editorial comments; they fueled me to the finish line! I want to give a very special thanks to my wife Jan Raynaud who tirelessly stood by my side, reading every word over, and over. Her dedication, commitment, and encouragement made "Healing Rain" possible. I Love you Jan!

Other Books by Fred Raynaud

The Seers Gift
A Look at the Language of Visions & Dreams

The Seer & Healing
The Seer Gift and the Ministry of Healing

The Seer & Prophecy
The Gift & Office of the Seer Prophet

The Seer's Guide to Symbolism
Similitudes, Metaphors, & Symbolism

The Eyes of a Chef
Kitchen Tales on Food & Faith

The Chef Architect
Concept Development & Design

"...His going forth is prepared as the morning; and he shall come unto us as the rain, as the latter and former rain unto the earth."

–HOSEA 6:3, KJV

1 PROLOGUE

I was only 20, but I felt 40. War, violence, and persecution, has a way of aging you. I do remember a little
of the peaceful years. I was six when the first wave
came across the southwest border. I didn't understand it
at the time—it was frightening. In 2014, the terrorist
group ISIS slaughtered people and took over villages in
Syria and Iraq. The beheadings started soon after. The
world watched in horror, as two Western journalists, along
with one aid worker, were brutally killed over live TV.
ISIS vowed it would not stop until they created a caliphate governed by strict Sharia law. Their target: The
West.

After the beheading of an Australian dignitary, ISIS teams made their way across the U.S. border. In 2017, the first slaughter took place at a large ranch located in Texas. ISIS attacked three other ranches. Laborers, hiding out in a barn, defended the ranch and gunned down the terrorists. The nation raged in an uproar. People spoke out against the federal government for not protecting its citizens and closing the border. The following year the war began. Two nuclear bombs struck the U.S. and Israel. The response was devastating. Marshall Law ensued.

My dad told me, many in America feared a socialist infiltration under the Obama administration. The economy never recovered. To offset the government mindset, the pendulum swung in the other direction. The real enemy: Fascism. Under the Damien administration, all hell broke loose.

In my teens, we feared for our existence. A thick darkness fell across the land. People disappeared from their homes, were imprisoned, and forced into government rehabilitation centers and labor camps for no rhyme or reason. Damien targeted Christians—to him, they were synonymous with crazy violent militias.

The darkness continued. The cries of the remnant became louder and louder... until seven voices of thunder echoed across the land—seven loud and powerful voices, challenging the hearts of men and government. Some, called them prophets of doom, others, called them pinna-

cles of peace, but we called them the Sons of Thunder—
forerunners of Almighty God—the guardians of our time.
They are the tip-of-the-spear of the Lord, executing His
hand upon a planet gone mad. They are the glue—holding
together the distressed and downtrodden. They are the
fuel igniting the Fire of God, in proclamation of redemption and healing of the nations. In their proclamation,
waves of God's grace were released, washing many in the
love of the Lamb.

The weapons of these mighty ones were not of men;
they understood the love of the Father and the power of
saving grace. Their mantel: Peace. Their sword of truth
was fueled by love. In their hearts dwelt the power of redemption, hope, and freedom. In purity, they released the
Kingdom of Heaven upon the land, creating Cities of Refuge, in their wake.

Here we are, five years later, and chances are, if you are
reading this story, you know the struggle, and how we
came to be at this place in history. Ah, but enough of me,
I need to get to the heart of the matter.

The first time I met Mrs. Sara Parker Rosen was in the
summer of 24. I arrived at the little waterfront community
of Pelican Bay on August 21. Pelican Bay, located on the
north side of Santa Maria Island, is one of eight barrier
keys on Florida's west coast. This quaint coastal town had
an air of simple pride and timeless charm. A small marina
anchored the south side of town. At the end of Sara's

street stretched the historical city pier—built in 1911 as a dock for excursion trips, day boats from Tampa and St. Petersburg, and steamer ships bringing in supplies. That 678 foot pier withstood hurricanes and lesser storms, too numerous to mention. And, like Sara, parts of the pier had been damaged by storms—but always restored to its original condition.

Sara's beachfront cottage lay at the other end of the street, anchored to the blue waters of the Gulf of Mexico. The architecture of Pelican Bay is old Key West. Pastel colors framed beachfront cottages and 20th century homes, rough and worn from ocean air. The Rosen house, originally built in 1913, had a soft yellow exterior, trimmed in chipped white paint. It had a wrap-around porch, stretching from the front and extending to the back, overlooking the Gulf. In her driveway was a dust-covered, 1966 VW bus, with the words "Methuselah III" engraved in the rear wooden bumper. Cabbage palms, sea grapes, and saw palmettos anchored each side of her home. Sand dunes covered with long railroad vines spread out like fingers, sheltering the entrance to the Gulf. Gentle paths maneuvered through the dunes and around protected sea turtle nests to the beach ahead.

I was struck by the moment—seeing such tranquility amidst the destruction of our day. Watching the sea oats and grasses sway in the wind, brought a mysterious peace, to the beauty of the calm blue waters. It was refreshing to see a town so peaceful and true to its origins. But what should I have expected? It was, after all, the first City of Refuge.

My name is James McEnroe. I write for an underground blog, called: The Remnant. The same name we use to describe ourselves. We are survivors in a world gone mad. The good news: we are growing, and in the end we will be more than a remnant.

It was 8:00 AM when I knocked on the door.

I was greeted by an aged-tender smile. "Well you must be James. Bless you, and welcome! My name is Nikita. Sara is out back. She's expecting you."

"She knows I'm here?"

Nikita stared at me with a bright wrinkly smile. "Of course, James. Papa told her you were coming this morning. She got up real early and brushed her hair. Go on; she's out back waiting."

"Yes Ma'am."

"Oh, one more thing Mr. McEnroe..."

"Yes Ma'am?"

"Don't call me Ma'am, I am not... that old you know. I like your work—quite a talented young man. We are blessed to have you. All my friends call me Nikita, or Niki, if it's easier to remember," she said with a wink and a smile.

Her wink caught me off guard; I chuckled, almost tripping over a tub of water sitting on the porch next to the front door. It had a blue and white hand painted sign above it reading, "Sandy toes here, please."

"This way?" I asked.

Nikita nodded.

I made my way around an old weathered swing and turned the corner towards the back porch. I saw Sara rocking in a white wicker chair, gazing out at the water. *"She's not as frail as I imagined for a woman in her eight-ies,"* I thought. Her long gray hair was tied back with a shell comb and a long blue ribbon. It gave her a youthful appearance. A breeze blew across her face, revealing soft, gray eyes.

She turned and said, "Come over here James, don't be afraid. I promise I won't bite."

"Yes Ma'am."

"Well, I suppose we have a lot to talk about."

"That's my prayer, Mrs. Rosen."

"Please, call me Sara."

"Sara, I was hoping we could talk about your life... and John's amazing history."

"Ah, yes. My Johnny."

"Sara, I want to tell your story. I want to write it out, as it happened. With your permission, I would like to journal the story of the Rain King. I want to send it out to the remnant, to those who have not heard the voice of our God. I know it will reach and comfort many."

"I see," she said, pausing for a moment to stare out at the Gulf. "Well then, we better get to it. It's a long story, I hope you can stay for a bit," she said, smiling.

"That's music to my ears! As long as it takes, if you don't mind having me around."

"Not at all James, we're glad to have you here.... Besides, Papa gave me a green light.... He said, 'Tell it all. Tell it from the beginning, just as it happened.' So, here we are. Would you like a cold glass of ginger green tea, or sweet? We have both."

That was the day I met Mrs. Sara Parker Rosen.... So, the story I am about to tell you is true, and I wrote it, just as she told me. She says some things are fuzzy. But I know different, Sara is sharp as a tack, and her reflections of those years were so real to her, I found myself swept away, as she shared.

This is the story of Sara, and her son John. This is an epic of one mother's will to survive, and believe, and one man's journey towards destiny. This is the story of the Rain King, one of seven voices, crying out in the wilderness—prepare for the coming of the King.

2 Shadows

July 11, 1980

Her bare feet dug into the floor mat. She pressed hard on the pedal, "Owwwww! Oh my GOD...." The pain kept coming... throbbing pain... faster, and STRONGER. It shot through Sara's lower back, with sharp, rhythmic force—the maternal cry of a body, too old for child bearing—too old to bring a life into this world. "Please Jesus, not here, not now," tears began to flow again, "HELP me!" The pain intensified. Her soft grey eyes swelled, as tears formed swollen pockets under her skin.

"Aaaaahhh!" she gripped the wheel. Her head slammed against the back of her hands. Spasmodic contractions threw Sara forward. She was spinning from the force of the impact. Dazed, all she sensed was the smell of burning rubber, and the sound of silent prayers mingled with the pounding rain. Loud echoing drops, beat to the tempo of her pain.

"*I shouldn't be driving,*" she thought, "*but I need to get home. It's been thirty years....*" Her mind wondered, "*I bet its boarded up—cobwebs everywhere.*" She remembered swinging on the front porch, in her mother's arms. "*I miss her comfort. She always told me what I should do.*" She thought about the despair on her mother's face, the brokenness and fear that haunted her.

Sara drew upon her mother's strength the day she ran away. Behind her mother's broken face and tear-filled eyes, was a voice that told Sara to **run**... *run and never stop.* Her beaten down gaze penetrated Sara's heart. Over time, that silent cry became Sara's strength. Her mother pleaded, "Go—go now! Run—keep on running, and NEVER come back! Do you UNDERSTAND ME SARA? NEVER!" Sara did. She got away.

Those words became the backbone to Sara's survival. At fourteen, it pushed her past, the grass-lined dirt road leading away from her Midwest home. It drove her from the horrifying memories of her stepfather; she tried to forget, but the scars remained. She drew on that strength in her twenties, surviving New Orleans street-life. The Big Easy... is not so easy, when you're a working girl, on the corner of Tulane Avenue—it's dangerous! Yet, in spite of the pain and the shame, scar upon scar, she kept moving forward.

Her mother's words held her, when her husband died in her arms. She wanted to run—she was running still. *"Momma, you would have loved him. You'd be proud of me. I miss him so much!"* She fought her contractions. Her thoughts drifted to the pulse of the rain. They kept coming in rhythmic cadence, as flashes of lightning cut through the sky like jagged wedges of light... piercing the outer darkness.

Sara left New Orleans in the 70s and headed north to Meridian Mississippi, landing a job as a server at the historic Weidmann's Restaurant, off I-20. She met Todd in the winter of 78. She never trusted men, hadn't loved anyone, and by no means did she let her guard down, to release her *true* self. *"Todd was different,"* she thought. He was an honest simple man with a pure heart. It didn't take long for the walls of bitterness, shame, and distrust, to start breaking down. She had fallen in love. Their marriage happened fast. In three months, they went from a love/fear relationship... to a fairytale marriage; for the first time, Sara understood what it meant to be "loved" by a man, with no conditions.

To onlookers, Todd was intimidating. At 6' 2", with the build of a running back, and the reach of a boxer, it is easy to understand why. In truth, he had a quiet disposition. When he spoke—he was present. He'd look you in the eye, like you were the only one in the room. His physique matched his strong moral fiber. Todd was a Christian man with faith and conviction—but never overpowering. He had one desire: to love his new wife and help her mend the pain of her past. He understood that Jesus was the only one who could touch a place that deep... that sore... that tender... and He did.

It happened on their honeymoon, in Destin Florida. Sara woke up early and went for a walk on the beach. She loved the beach—the sound of the waves, the salt-scented breeze, and the sugar-white sand, gave her peace. "My new home—Florida. I like the sound of that! Way better, than that dusty old house."

Love and marriage were new to Sara. It was amazing to be comforted and at peace. Love's touch opened her heart to new thoughts and emotions. Still, with this newness, came a flood of memories—buried deep inside.

When you open up your heart, things begin to happen—memories rise up—numbness fades. Ugly memories from Sara's childhood floated to the surface. She kept walking, kicking sand in the air, as she wrestled with a stream of emotions. Her walk turned to a pace. Her pace turned to panic. Back and forth she retraced her steps, digging a path in the sand with her toes. The silent cleansing of turquoise waves washed away her steps, but not the memories. She stared down at the sea-foam fading into the receding pull of the tide. She wanted her past to wash away too. She stopped and crouched down, "God, I don't think I can take it anymore. Please, help me!" Kneeling like a beach ball in the sand, she rocked back and forth, remembering her abuser—the nights of paralyzing fear.

Tears started flowing again. Anger rose up in her heart and mind. Her childhood had been stripped away. "Why me God... why me?" Like two opposing forces, Sara's feelings collided. She believed God was a God of love, or so she thought. Abused as a child, a prostitute in her twenties, and now she struggled with *the need* to be healed and forgiven. It was overwhelming.

Yet, Todd's heart drew her. Sara tried to push him away, "God may love you Todd, but He doesn't know me. I'm not a good person! He could never love me as much as he loves you."

Todd hung in there. He showed up at Weidmann's every day at 11:00 AM and ordered the same thing, a slice (or two) of their famous black-bottom pie. He loved the crust; they made it with crushed gingersnaps and butter. The best part: a thick creamy layer of bourbon-laced chocolate. With fork in hand and a smile on his face, he made the same offer, "Eat dinner with me Sara? We're meant to be together." When she ignored him, he would order another slice of pie, and ask again, "Come on Sara; let's grab a bite... *or maybe just a cup of coffee?*"

She gave in. That dinner date became a seed, fostering a new direction for Sara. Seeing love's reflection in Todd's heart became therapeutic. *"So this is what love looks like,"* she thought.

Over the months, her heart softened. Now married, she sought the Lord with everything she had. God's love drew her. *"It must be God's hand in his life."* She was still hurting, *"Why did God allow this? How could He allow that beast to hurt me?"* Drowning in her pain, she cried out, "Jesus... **can you hear me?**"

Desperate, sitting in the sand, she could hear Todd's voice whispering in the back of her mind, *"In the stillness of your heart, He will answer."* She stopped rocking. The sun began to rise and reflect upon the greenish blue of the water's horizon. Gulls started their morning procession along the surf. The daybreak's beauty quieted her soul. She began to speak to God from a new place—a place of whole heartedness, "Jesus... if you are real, please forgive me for my sins."

Then it happened; no sooner did she get to the "I" in "If," than the sweet presence of the Holy Spirit rested upon her. Waves of His love moved through her body—a pure experience beyond words. *"Peace,"* she thought,

"*Amazing...*" the weight of the past was lifting, "*...I feel whole for the first time.*" She was transported to a different place, beyond space and time. Everything became quiet. "*It's like floating in the warm sea of God's presence,*" she thought, "*I feel wrapped in His love.*" Moments became hours. Peace and joy filled her heart, "*Am I dreaming?*"

Sara saw herself from above, "*I'm a child,*" she thought. Her child-self stopped, and glanced up. Her eyes met Jesus.

He stared back with warmth and compassion, "Come child."

With arms wide open, she ran and leaped into his lap. She nudged her face into his neck, and whispered in his ear, "I love you so much."

The Lord embraced her, "I love you very much Sara."

Then, as if she knew something, she grabbed Him, and held on tight... "Someone's coming." She turned and stared beyond the pillars, into the outer darkness.... Fear struck her heart.

"What's wrong my child?" Jesus said with reassuring comfort and strength.

"I don't like what's out there—in the darkness. It's cold out there," she said trembling.

"Its okay child, nothing can harm you here, I promise!" His words flowed over her like a warm blanket.

"I know," she said, whimpering.

"Its alright, it's going to be okay—I'm with you...." His words quieted her spirit. He asked her, "Do you know what you must do?"

"Yes Lord, but I'm afraid," she said, squeezing him with all her might, "Don't let me go!"

As Sara peered into the darkness, a slow moving figure lurked forward. Its head was cast down, in shame and fear. A dark old man walked forward, cringing... hiding in the fog... unable to enter—until the light struck him.... "My God, it's my stepfather!"

Jesus responded, "Sara, is this the man?"

"Yes Lord," holding on even tighter.

Jesus stared at him. His eyes looked into his soul, "He'll never hurt you Sara... never again!"

He held her with his left hand; in his right: a golden scepter embedded with rubies forming a crown. Engraved on its side read the words of angels, "*en Logos ek Theos – Basileus Basileuo kai Kurios Kurieuo*," meaning: "The Word of God—the Sovereign, all Powerful King of Kings and Lord of all Lords." He pointed the scepter towards him. The old man fell to the ground.

With soft reassuring words, He said, "Sara, go ahead, you can do it.... Tell him."

Sara said, "I forgive you." Her own forgiveness released her.... She understood that this act of forgiveness... placed all judgment into the hands of Jesus. Sara experienced freedom for the first time.

Jesus embraced her, as he looked at this shadowed of a man. Then he waved his scepter towards him. The silence of his nod and the expression in his eyes said enough, *"Be gone from me... return to your holding cell until the time of my visitation."*

The man cowered back into the darkness, disappearing, then gone.

Sara was back in the arms of Jesus, only this time she was an adult. She sat comforted and embraced. It's ironic, she knew she loved Jesus her entire life, even though she just met him. She was in a state of restful sleep.

Sara came to, weightless like a feather. "Lord... what happened?" The heaviness lifted. Anger and rage disappeared. Something healed inside, *"This must have been a dream?"* Tears filled her eyes, "You're real! YOU'RE RE-ALLY REAL...." She wiped tears from the sides of her face. The hairs on her arms stood on end. An intense current moved through her.

God whispered to her spirit, *"I love you Sara...."*

In her mind's eye, Jesus wrapped his arms around her as waves of peace enveloped her. Sara knew what "being saved" meant. *"It's God's amazing love,"* she thought, *"too simple... saying uncle, surrendering... it isn't that hard after all. I feel like my eyes are open for the first time— I'm born-again."*

Todd's explanations about Christ, who He was, and what He did, came alive! *"He did this for me!"* she thought. "Todd? Oh my..." She got up and ran back to the beach house. *"Todd is going to flip out!"* she couldn't wait to tell him. In the twinkling of an eye her life had changed and Todd had to share in her newfound joy.

She stood at the side of the bed watching him sleep. Filled with Joy... she didn't know what to say, *"I'm free! But how do you explain something so incredible, so beautiful, and mysterious."*

She snuck into the covers and stroked his thick black hair and stubbed face with her fingernails. Looking at Todd, she began to tear-up again, "God thank you for bringing this man in my life!" The gentle comfort of the Holy Spirit rested upon her.

Todd opened his eyes, rolled over, and hugged his wife. "Hey sweetie, did you sleep okay?" his voice was soft. He squeezed her.

"Todd..." she whispered. His eyes closed again as he nestled in the comfort of her arms... "Todd... Honey... It happened."

"What happened?"

"Todd, I met Him...." Her heart pounded at the thought of Todd's joy.

"Who?" Todd muffled, "Who did you meet?"

"Jesus, silly, I met Jesus, just like you said. He came into my heart. I can't explain it. It's so real! He's so real."

Sara struggled to find the words to express what had taken place, how he healed the wounded child within her.

Todd, now wide-awake and sitting up in bed, wrapped his arms around her. "Tell me about it, what happened?"

Sara shared with Todd her beach experience.

Todd was amazed, "Thank you Lord." His prayers had been answered.

A pothole in the road lunged Sara back to the present. "*My neck hurts! This drive is tedious...*" she thought, "*It doesn't look like this storm is going to let up soon.*" The long drive up to the panhandle had taken its toll on Sara. Her baby jerked her into reality. Fear struck her heart. The thought of her water breaking at any moment was paralyzing. "*My baby!*" she thought, "Lord you promised." she began to pray... "*Harie auti auti harie, shando— shando rhama curease.*" Her prayers fused into a song of praise—in a language unknown to her, a gift of the Holy Spirit. As she prayed, her baby started to kick.

Sara rubbed her abdomen. She traced the outline of her baby's leg beneath her skin. The child's soft kicks caused Sara to reflect on the miracle, in her womb. She started reminiscing about the day she received the promise—the gift of a child.

Sara had explained to Todd why she couldn't bear children. "It is medically impossible Todd, I am scarred for life!"

Todd just said, "Don't worry Sara; with God all things are possible."

They were at a church service when she first received the promise. It happened when she least expected it. Todd and Sara walked into Living Streams Fellowship, seeking a night of worship with friends. The mood in the church was sweet and aromatic. The worship team sang songs of Holiness. The presence of God filled the place as if the wind of the Spirit was blowing and angels' wings were in the air.

With eyes closed and arms raised in praise to God, Todd began seeing pictures; visions of rain flooded his mind. Thick clouds of rain moved across the horizon. It was as if the hand of God was calling for rain, moving the clouds to a point of downpour. The Lord whispered to Todd:

"Ask for rain in the time of the latter rain and I the Lord shall make bright clouds, and give showers of rain to all that call upon My name!"

Todd, with stammering lips said, "Rain down on us Lord. Send us your rain. Wash us dear God—let it rain! Let your rain bring forth your kingdom reign."

The worship stopped and Todd, filled with the Holy Spirit, glanced over at Sara. She was trembling. The presence of the Holy Spirit was all over her. Her eyes fluttered and her amber hair was wet with perspiration, as if a mist had covered her with a blanket of sweet rain. "Honey, are you okay?"

"Yes," she said, "The Lord is all over me." It took Sara a moment to catch her breath and gain focus, "While we sang I was caught up in the Spirit, flying through the heavens... riding on the back of a white dove. It had talons like an eagle. We soared through the clouds with incredible strength and majesty. I watched the sky turn into a mass of thick dark clouds, ready to burst forth at any moment. I gazed down, I wasn't flying *into* the clouds; the dove *created* the clouds. They were flowing from the underside of his wings like billows of smoke. We soared around the heavens until the sky was dense with clouds. Then it happened, rain burst forth. The dove kept flying. Faster, and faster, we soared in the rain... everything became wet. Rain poured from his feathers, molting feathers bringing forth the latter rain of His presence. I was drenched in water. Then I came to, and... well... look at me, I'm all wet!" She stared at Todd, eyes fresh with sweet anointing.

Todd tried to make sense of it. "*Her wetness might be perspiration, but My God, she's all wet,*" he thought, "*Like heaven's mist...*" A Holy rain covered her. He shared with her his own experience and they sat praising God for His sweet touch. They kept quiet about Sara's mist experience and held it in their hearts.

"Life was different then," she thought as she headed towards I-10. The storm was a deluge. *"I wish this storm would let up! If I could just get to the interstate."* The wipers were riding on sheets of water. The windows fogged up. Visibility dissipated fast. Sara turned on the radio for a weather update but reception was terrible. Her contractions started again—a maternal clock ticking to the sound of the rain; she thought it might be tonight.

The promise spoken by Bo flooded her mind. She reflected on that night God spoke hope into their lives. They had gone to a workshop on "Listening to the voice of God." Bo Jackson was one of the speakers. He flew in from Kansas City. His home church experienced a tremendous revival and he was going to speak on the "Seeds of Revival." Bo was an older man with long gray hair and a salt and pepper beard that framed his aging face. He had light sky-blue eyes that seemed to see right through you. They said he was a prophet. God had been using Bo Jackson to plant seeds of revival at many churches throughout the South.

After his message, he stopped and stared at the crowd. He raised his hand up to heaven and said in a soft tone, "Holy Spirit come." Within seconds, the place was electrified as God's presence filled the Church. People were crying and praising God; others trembled and worshiped in quiet submission.

Bo gave a few prophetic words to several people, calling out strangers by name, speaking hope and encouragement into their lives. He stopped and gazed at Sara, "The lady in the tapestry dress..." pointing in Sara's direction, "Please stand up."

With hesitance, Sara stood.

"Is your name Sara?"

"Why yes—yes it is," she stuttered.

"And that big fellow next to you... is that your husband?"

"It is." Her mind was racing a million miles an hour.

"Please stand sir."

Todd stood and took hold of Sara's hand.

"Have the two of you been praying about something close to your hearts?"

They nodded in agreement.

"You have been praying for a miracle, haven't you?"

"Yes," Sara replied tearfully.

"The Lord wants me to tell you, he has answered your prayers. Your hearts have been ushered up into the heavens and your petition rose like incense before the Lord.... When I noticed the two of you in the audience I saw storm clouds' circling around you. Heaven's light was shining on you—blue and white lights of glory and revelation. The Lord said, 'the child you have been praying for will indeed be born. The womb you thought was dead will bring forth life.' The Lord on High—He is the resurrection and the life. He shall speak into your womb, remove the scars, and give you a child. The healing has begun! Even now, as I am speaking, the warmth of the Holy Spirit is on you; can you feel His presence?"

"Yes Sir."

"Child, that warmth you are experiencing... is the healing-touch from the Master's hand!"

"Todd, my abdomen—it's burning!" A creative miracle was taking place. She knew she was healed. God was giving her the ability to have children.

"God wants you to know that you will conceive and have a son. With tremendous grace, God will use this boy for His glory. I heard the Lord say, '*I shall use him to bring forth my Word. It will come as a mighty rain upon the land. He shall be a Rain King in the arsenal of my quiver. I shall cause him to call forth the latter rain of my presence and bring showers upon dry and desolate lands. The time of my coming is approaching. It will be a day unlike any day before it. Healing rain shall fall.... It will be a season of the Latter Rain—a time of great harvest... and a season of separation in the land.*'"

With sadness in his eyes, he said, "But in pain you shall conceive and sorrow will fill your heart, but only for a season. Do not despair my child, for I am with you, and my hand will be upon you. When the enemy rises up like a storm against you, know that I am your shield and your rear guard.... Do not fear... look up, your redemption is drawing near."

Then Bo said, "Take this scripture and know the King is with you:

"For I will pour water on the thirsty land, and streams on the dry ground; I will pour out My Spirit on your offspring, and My blessing on your descendants. They will spring up like grass in a meadow, like poplar trees by flowing streams."

-Isaiah 44:3–4, NIV

Bo remembered the prophetic words spoken by the 1934 U.K. revivalist, Arthur Burt:

"It shall come as a breath,
And the breath shall bring the wind,
And the wind shall bring the rain.
And there shall be floods, and floods, and floods,
And torrents, and torrents, and torrents,
Souls shall be saved like falling leaves from mighty oaks
swept by a hurricane.
Arms and legs shall come down from Heaven,
And there shall be no ebb."

He stopped for a moment, assessed the pulse of the crowd, then said, "Let's stand and ask our Father to wake up our souls, and shake off our outer garments. Let's prepare our hearts for the rain." A heavenly silence fell, as a spirit of worship moved through the crowd.

Sara remembered that moment as if it were yesterday. The baby in her womb was a living promise—on the verge of becoming a reality. Remembering that promise, and the visions of rain, while being stuck in this downpour, seemed so ironic.

As she drove, Sara recalled the day she confirmed being pregnant. It was the spring of 79, on their six-month anniversary. "I'm going to have a baby?" she asked the doctor, "But they told me I could never have children...."

"I cannot speak to that, Sara. All I know, is you're going to have a baby. And as for the damage to your uterus, you're in perfect health, no scar tissue whatsoever."

"They were wrong doctor! God is so good!"

"I suppose he is Sara, a baby is a very precious gift."

She sang, as she lit two candles to frame the flowers on the dining room table. Sara waited for Todd to come home. She was so excited to share the good news with him.

But, Todd never arrived. Her good news was overshadowed by the sound of the phone ringing and the voice on the other end, "Mrs. Parker? Is this Mrs. Sara Parker, wife of a Mr. Todd Parker?"

"Yes.... Can I help you? Has something happen? Where's Todd? Is it Todd?"

"Mrs. Parker... This is Father Donavan; I'm with the Trauma unit at Grace General Hospital. It's your husband... he's been in an accident. We need you down here now!"

"Is he ok? ...Tell me what's wrong!" Panic set in, her heart was racing.... Tears began to swell as her silent pleas to Jesus, went up to heaven.

"Please hurry Ma'am!" The sound of his voice was frightening.

"Oh my God..." Sara's face went flush. She held back the tears that strangled her ability to speak. She panicked in her effort to get in the car and drive to the hospital.

The ride was a daze... every moment spent fighting tears and fears with petitions to God for his healing grace. When she arrived at the hospital, there was no place to park. She drove around the block, and then drove the car into the grass, leaving it there, with the engine running. Then, she ran into the ER.

She asked the receptionist, "My husband... there's been an accident! His name is Todd Parker.... Excuse me! I NEED TO SEE MY HUSBAND!"

Father Donavan was standing nearby, waiting for Sara. He walked up and introduced himself, "I'm Father Donavan. Are you Mrs. Parker?"

"Yes, I am. Can you take me to my husband?"

"Come with me dear, I will take you to him." He placed his arm around her shoulder and led her to the elevator; "We're going to the trauma center on the third floor... We're almost there. Hold on dear." Sara's body was shaking.

Father Donavan escorted Sara to a private waiting room. "Stay here and I'll get you in to see him."

Sara was in a state of complete shock.

Another priest entered the room, "I'll stay with you dear. My name is Father Jonathan... we'll get you right in, I promise."

Sara sat on the sofa, broken. She was quivering. She couldn't breathe. Jonathan put his arm around her. "We can see him now."

They walked down the corridor to a door that led them to the trauma wing. Hitting the buzzer to gain access they went through the doors. The wing was lined with glass-enclosed rooms on the left and a long nurse's station on the right. The floor had an unforgettable smell... a medicinal smell that lingered in the air. The tile walkway went on forever. The paintings on the wall flashed by, like bill-boards on a highway. Everything moved in slow motion. The world stopped—she couldn't move. Father Jonathan helped her along.

She found Todd lying in bed with bandages around his head and machines hooked up on both sides. A nurse standing at the foot of his bed greeted her.

Sara walked up and grabbed hold of his hand... he was motionless.... She was afraid she was going to hurt him, "Todd... baby... you're going to be fine... I love you honey... Todd, sweetie... you have to be ok! You're going to be a daddy. Honey...." She cried resting her head on his chest. His heart beat to the rhythm of the oxygen being forced into his lungs. His body was warm, almost hot... and his breathing loud. His eyes were closed and all she saw was his beauty. Every detail stood out: his black lashes and thick eyebrows, the scar on his arm, his chin and cheek bones. "Sweetie... wake-up, please!"

The priest stood by to comfort her. In slow motion, she turned her head to the nurse, tears rolling down her cheeks, "What happened to him? What is going on?"

"Mrs. Parker, he's been in a terrible accident with a serious trauma inflected on his brain. The doctor is on his way here, he will give you more information."

A sheriff entered the room. "Hello... Mrs. Parker?" he said, "My name is Detective Stevens. I'm investigating your husband's accident. I am so sorry.... I'll be down the hall. When you're ready, I will answer any questions you have."

"Investigate? What is going on? What happened to my husband?" Sara was numb, confused, and angered by the events. "Tell me what happened!" she said, as she squeezed Todd's hand in desperation.

"Mrs. Parker, please have a seat," he said, as Father Jonathan pushed a chair towards Sara.

"Tell me... I need to know!"

"From what we know at this time, your husband, Mr. Parker, was at a convenience store down on 5th street at about 6:30 PM, buying flowers. It appears that while he was in the store, a gunman entered the premise attempting to rob the cashier. A scuffle took place... gunfire ensued, and your husband jumped in front of a child to shield her. He saved her life. In the process, he was struck in the head. The gunman fled the scene and we're trying to locate him as we speak." Detective Stevens, was shaken, staring into Sara's eyes, "I am so sorry Mrs. Parker that's all I have right now."

The doctor arrived, "Mrs. Parker, I am Doctor Nasaki, head of Neurosurgery here at the hospital." Shaking her hand he said, "Here's what we have: Your husband obtained a serious injury to the lower quadrant of his brain. It severed his brain stem and damaged a good portion of his brain. The area of the brain struck governs thought process as well as motor functions. We have been running tests since he arrived and have concluded that he is brain dead."

"Brain dead! What does that mean?"

"There's no activity in the brain, the stem is severed. We ran a battery of tests—there is no brain activity." The doctor continued, "The state of Florida requires conformation from at least two physicians to determine whether someone is considered brain dead. We called in two other specialists to confirm our findings and should have more information for you in a few hours. I assure you Mrs. Parker we are doing everything possible. In the meantime, we have your husband on a breathing machine and we are monitoring all his vitals."

Paralyzed by the news, Sara's heart broke. In complete shock she cried, "Why God Why?" She held on to Todd not wanting to let go. Confusion set in, *"I thought you were in a coma... I thought you would come to."*

Minutes turned to hours as Sara sat by his side. It was all a blur—she didn't understand why this happened. Father Donavan entered the room and asked Sara if she wanted something to eat or drink. She shook her head in a daze....

She leaned over to Todd and rested her head on his chest, "Darling, you're going to be okay." She wiped his forehead with a damp cloth. "Todd, can you hear me? Honey, Wake-up please, wake-up now. We need you." She rested her head again and dosed off. She fell asleep—

exhausted by the trauma. She dreamt of her childhood—her mother rocking her on the front porch, holding her and telling her it's going to be all right. She dreamt about that song her mother used to sing to her as a child, "Jesus loves the little children—all the children of the world." She dreamt of Todd seated on the front porch next to her mother, drinking sweet tea and watching her baby in the arms of his grandmother. She pictured Todd reaching out and grasping the baby's hand, feeling the texture and smallness of his fingers. She saw Todd hugging their child and embracing him with so much love. Her dreams were soothing—much more than the present reality.

Todd passed away in the night while Sara slept... holding his hand. "Todd! Mommy—Jesus—*please*, help me." All she could do was cry. Her mind was attacked by feelings of complete and utter despair. Sara was gripped by fear, loneliness, anger, and deep sorrow: She felt paralyzed.

The days turned into weeks, and the weeks into months. She entered every stage of grief imaginable. She bounced back and forth between stages, trying to survive... or not... she didn't care. Still, she pressed on! With every step she took, the Lord gave her strength. The baby inside her was growing. She was alive with the seed of their marriage. All she had left was that piece of Todd living and growing within her.

Now, driving in the rain, she was trying to get back to a home that only existed in the slanted memories of her past. She was struck with this overpowering fear of loneliness. She didn't think she was going to make it. The contractions got stronger and the storm wasn't letting up.

She heard voices—dark whispers in the night. Something lurked in the shadows. She imagined seeing dark figures darting between flashes of lightening in the trees. Voices were telling her to end it, to move on, to join her husband—life was not worth living! She tried to pray but the depression intensified.

Sara heard a loud crack of thunder, sending her into panic. She turned left, then right, trying to stop. Her car was out of control, spinning and sliding in the rain. "Oh my God... Oh GOD!" she cried, "My baby... My Baby... PLEASE!" Sara screamed at the top of her lungs. Tires screeched. The rain, lightning, and thunder intensified. She hit the brakes again and held on to her stomach with both hands.

"BAM!" Sara's car struck a tree. The front end of the vehicle wrapped itself around an oak, like foil. Moments earlier the tree was struck by lightning. It was in flames. The force of the crash lodged Sara between the steering wheel, just below her breasts and the seat, missing the baby by inches. Her knees wedged into the dash. The street was covered with broken glass. The engine revved with a high screeching sound, as if it was stuck in high gear...

then died. The rain kept coming down. The tree smoked and smoldered. Sara moved in and out of consciousness, her face bruised and swollen from the impact. In all this chaos, she still clung to her abdomen, forming a protective shield around her baby. She felt her baby coming, as he kicked into position. With her head cut... and bleeding down the sides of her face, she cried out to God, "Help me!"

The contractions grew harder. Sara knew her water might break at any moment ... and it did. She clenched her sides and bore down to push. Her chest was bruised. Her neck was bent into the back of the seat. Trapped in the twisted rubble of the car, she kept pushing, crying with all her heart, "Please God PLEASE... Protect my baby!" Sara pushed, and screamed, and pushed again, falling in and out of a state of consciousness, then she passed out. The only sound heard... was the sound of a baby crying... to the backdrop of the rain. The downpour of the storm continued as the baby's cry echoed through the night.

3 WINGS

From inside the wreckage prowled a shadowy creature—a fallen beast from the underworld. A demon of torment hovered behind Sara. His task was almost complete. "When I get done with her, she will be gone for good!" He passed through the twisted iron, slashing the gas line with his talon, then laughed, mocking God, as he slithered away from Sara and her child. "Dharana, Dharana!" the demon shouted, "Dharana will be exalted in the tribunals of my master... I destroyed the plans of the Most High. They will worship Meee!"

Out of nowhere, a flash of brilliant golden light, as hot as the white coals glowing from Heaven's alter, illuminated the back of the creature.

"Noooo..." Dharana wheezed, "She's mine, the baby is mine. You're too late—the woman will not live to see daylight." The demon stumbled backwards, scrambling to get out of the light and away from Nathan the Heavenly warrior.

"Not today, fallen creature. The Lord of Heaven rebukes you!" Nathan removed his silver light sword from its sheath and swung, "*Slash... slash...*" slicing across the spineless back of Dharana as he attempted to run away. The force sent him flying—spinning across the road. "Be gone you." But, before Nathan could finish, Dharana slithered off the road leaving a trail of green pus behind.

Nathan stood there, tall and brilliant, with penetrating green eyes framed by the long golden locks that rested on his massive shoulders. He peered into the wreckage at Sara and her child. Sara's body was trapped between the floor, the seat, and the wheel.

Nathan reached between the twisted metal and pushed the front seat into the rear. He took hold of the baby and eased it out from the warmth of his mother. Sara was unconscious. Nathan severed the baby's cord, and wiped away the embryonic fluid that clung to the baby's eyes and nose. He placed his hand on the baby's head and said, "Health to you child, health in the name of the King." A warm energy flowed from his hand into the baby. He called for one of his scouts, "Cayla, come, take the child." Nathan handed the baby to a tall slender angel. Cayla had a bluish glow around him with a pale muscular body and the physique of a long distance runner. His elegant flowing white wings covered his massive arms. He nested the baby under the warmth of his wing.

At various strategic locations around the wreckage stood a team of Angelic Guardians. They setup a perimeter of light to protect the child and Sara.

Nathan reached in, and slid Sara out and onto the ground. He took the child from Cayla and embraced it, kissed it, and blessed it in the name of the Most High. "So much pain, so much damage. Is it time Lord?" he asked the Father.

"Not yet Nathan, the time is coming soon," the soothing voice of Jesus filled his mind—then silence. The rain stopped and the sky started to clear.

"Cayla, take the child to Daniel and Nikita—the intercessors at Pelican Bay. The Lord is preparing their hearts for your arrival. Raphael will join you soon. I am staying with Sara until she is safe in the hands of physicians. Go now, be on alert, the forces of darkness will not stop until they have killed the child."

Cayla embraced the child under his wing, and with the speed and force greater than the wind, he spun into the night, escorted by two Holy Guardians.

"Oh God... God... *Shando rhama kurea au... Father... etea naa na rhamas sta.* Jesus, JESUS... What does it mean Lord? *Shando na... Shando na...*" Daniel, raptured in God's presence, prayed in his prayer language. His words cut through the air like swords of fire. His heart pounded.

He sat at the edge of the bed, hypnotized by a dream, that moments earlier awakened him, his face luminous with the presence of God. Daniel glanced over his shoulder at Nikita. His gaze moved beyond the tranquility of her sleep.

Daniel walked to their old cedar chest, sat down and stared out the window, "*4:08, I can't believe it,*" he thought, "*It must have rained last night.*" The late-night fog clung to the window, blanketing the alcove in front of their house. His window overlooked Pelican Bay. The calm waters of Florida captured his soul.

Daniel gazed through a hole cut away in the clouds and stared at the stars. His thoughts ran from one dimension to another, replaying that incredible dream.

Nikita woke moments earlier. She watched her husband staring out the window of their moon lit room. She reached for him resting her hand on his shoulder, "Are you okay?"

His thoughts were a thousand miles from home. He replied, "I had the strangest dream last night."

"Tell me about it," she said. Nikita was stunning, with her shoulder length curly hair and chocolate skin from too much sun. Her eyes were light blue, almost white, and when she smiled, it lit up the room.

"I saw angels fighting the forces of darkness. Their swords clashed—sending out beams of dazzling white light that wiped out the enemy."

"Are you okay?" Nikita knew Danny well. They had been together for 8 years: young lovers at the age of twenty. They met on the West Coast, in San Diego California. She was on spring break, enjoying the fun and frolic of beach life, 2,000 miles from home. Daniel was your typical surfer dude. At first glance, you'd think he was a Rastafarian. He had long sun-bleached dreadlocks, tied at the top of his head and extended down the center of his back. He had a thumb size goatee below his lower lip, a tattoo of a chef's knife woven with fresh herbs on the inside of his right arm, and a tattoo of a driftwood cross anchored by two angel's wings on the back of his neck. Daniel was a chef by trade. They owned their own little restaurant called "The Rusty Bus," named after their old 66 VW Westphalia.

Holding his wife's hand, he said, "Nikita, the battle was so real." He knew the war between the dominion of darkness and the Kingdom of Heaven was raging... and humanity was trapped in the middle. "Babe, we joined this fight for a reason.... God has a higher purpose for us!"

She sat back in the rocker, knowing the reality of what he said, "Danny, let's pray!"

Together they began to pray.... Deeper and deeper they prayed, until all had dissipated, and the sweet aroma of the Lord, filled the upper room of their home.

Nikita started worshiping. She reached up in a symbolic move of breaking through the heavens. A vision began to fill her mind.... In her vision, she saw herself staring at the front door.... Then she heard a knock... and went to answer it. When she opened the door, a blazing red and silver light, like the fire of a sunset, illuminated her. The white silhouette of a figure, approached. She knew in her spirit, it was an angel. As the angel came closer, it became brighter and clearer—more in focus. She saw a bundle in its arms... "It's a baby," she whispered. The vision faded. Nikita sat galvanized, "Wow, my God... that was powerful!"

"Nikita, what happened?"

She told Danny about the vision. Together they sought the Lord... searching for a meaning.

The Spirit of God spoke to Daniel, "The vision is true!' When the sun breaks across the horizon, you will hear a knock at the door. When you open it, you will find a baby, wrapped in a blanket, lying in a basket. ...Take this child and care for him, until the day he is reunited with his mother."

"Oh my God, Danny, what are we going to do?"

"Nikita, there's more…. The Holy Spirit said the baby's name is John. He has a great need for this child. We are to protect him… and nurture him. Then He said, continue praying… the times are changing quickly."

They sat in their room, staring out the window, in silence—waiting for the sun to rise. The light of the moon reflected on the water beyond their house.

Soon, the sun began to arise above the mangroves. They heard a noise—it was a knock. They sat for a moment, motionless—not believing their ears.

"You think?" Daniel whispered.

Nikita poked Danny's knee with her finger, "Go…. Hurry, see who it is."

"Nikita… I hear a baby crying…. Did you hear that?"

Together they rushed down the stairs and hurried to the door. They stared at each other, and then smiled, hearts pounding in anticipation. They opened the door and looked down. Just as the Lord had spoken, peering between the crevices of a bundled up blanket, were two small, deep blue eyes. "It's a newborn," Nikita said. They looked around for onlookers—hoping to catch a glimpse of an angel.

Unbeknownst to them, two invisible guardian angels positioned themselves on the roof of their house, watching for any sign of the enemy.

Nikita reached down and picked up the child.

Daniel took hold of the basket and rushed back into the house. The streets of Pelican Bay were quiet. The town was still asleep.

Nikita sat on the sofa and rested little John on her lap. She removed the blanket, and said, "Oh my, Daniel... what are we going to do?" She wiped the baby's face with a tissue. He began to cry—hungry—in search for the comfort of its mother.

4 THIRD HEAVEN

Nathan placed his sword on the ground, and kneeled between Sara and the wreckage. Then the car exploded, fire and debris flew in all directions. Nathan raised his wings, shielding Sara's body from the blaze. The flames from the wreckage shot across the back of his wings, leaving a trail of grayish black soot. Nathan held Sara's unconscious body on his lap and began to rub her head with his fingers. Her pulse was weak. She was breathing heavy and had no movement in her eyes. *"What did that imp do?"* He thought. With affection, he whispered into Sara's spirit, "Dear child of God... you're going to live... and not die." He picked her up and carried her further away from the car. Then sat down next to her while he waited for Raphael, one of his lieutenants, to arrive.

About 20 miles north of the accident, outside the little town of Shady Grove, at an old 76 gas station, Raphael entered the station wagon of a family, in route to I-10. *"Ah, the perfect family, I hope they don't mind if I ride along."* Raphael had been dispatched to find someone, whose heart was right before God, to assist in Sara's rescue.

Henry and Barbara—the occupants of the car—had no idea of Raphael's presence. He seated himself behind Henry, maintaining an invisible state. Raphael leaned over and whispered into the mind of Henry, "*When you get to the street you must turn left...*"

Unsure of himself, Henry said to Barbara, "Honey, I think I know a short cut." He turned left, instead of right, and head in the wrong direction.

Barbara, preoccupied with an article in Reader's Digest, said, "Whatever you say dear, just don't get us lost again."

Raphael leaned over, and whispered again, "*It's getting late... you should speed up slightly.*"

Henry pressed on the gas pedal and took off down the highway—in the opposite direction of I-10. Raphael smiled and blessed them with a measure of peace and joy. They drove for several minutes discussing their trip and eagerness to get their vacation started. The car raced down the highway. They approached a hill that was hiding Sara's flaming car from their vision. Raphael reached over to Henry and touched the back of his neck... whispering, *"Slow down now.... The roads are slippery.... Be on the lookout.... The streets are not well lit."*

Chills ran down the back of Henry's neck and arms. Startled by what felt like a cool breeze, he turned to his wife, their eyes met, "Honey, did you..."

She interrupted him, "Slow down Henry! It's dark and slippery out there."

"Yes dear, I.... Oh, never mind...." He pressed down on the brakes and made his way up the hill towards the accident.

"Barbara, did you see that?" Henry pointed beyond the top of the hill along the tree line, "Something's flashing... over there..."

"Slow down Henry. I saw it." The accident was now in full view.

"Barbara, over there! The car is on fire!!"

"My God... I hope no one's hurt?" said Barbara.

"I'm going to stop.... Barbara, grab the mobile phone in my bag." Henry pulled off the road, parking across from the car. It was dark outside. An orange glow emanating from the flames lit the accident scene. Scattered pieces of smoldering plastic and twisted metal were everywhere.

Raphael exited the wagon and approached Nathan, "They're here... she's in good hands."

Nathan turned towards Raphael, "Put out the fire."

Raphael faced the car. With his massive wings outstretched, he smothered the flames with his body.

"Good job my friend—now we enter a new phase in this mission."

Henry stood astonished. He wondered why the fire went out—"Poof" it was gone, as if an invisible blanket suffocated the fire. Smoldering smoke bellowed out of the car turning the air into a gray cloudy mist. He glanced around, trying to find something... but what, he didn't know. "Barbara LOOK, over there... a body. Call 911 now." Henry was part of a fire-response unit and was testing a new analog mobile phone system for his department. "Barb, grab a blanket out of the wagon. I need something to brace her head."

Henry examined Sara. He checked for a pulse and listened to her breathing. Then placed a rolled up blanket around her head.

Raphael called out to Nathan, "The sophar has sounded. Has a tribunal been called?"

"Yes my friend. It's been blowing for a while now. Stay with Sara and ensure her safety. Take two Guardians with you and position them within the corridors of the hospital. You stay with Sara. Do not show yourselves, concealment is essential. Remember, stay by her side, until you receive further instructions."

The sophar was still sounding when Nathan stood to his feet, "I must go. I'm being summoned to the courts of the King." He smiled at Raphael and said, "Farewell mighty one, our King is with you!"

"Also with you my friend... also with you."

With that, Nathan picked up his sword and sheathed it. With arms lifted upwards and wings positioned at his side, he shot through the sky and into the blueness of the outer heavens.

5 COURTS OF THE KING

Flashes of lightening merged with the pounding of thunder, as the loud echoing sound of the sophar vibrated throughout the Third Heaven, and into the ears of all the Heavenly Host, stationed on Earth. A mighty Seraph stood on the platform of crystal, blowing a sophar—a golden horn used to call out the commands of Him who sits on the Throne. Depending on its melody, it would be either a sound of blessing, release, or summons, this time, a summons, calling the Captains of the Lord of Host to the war room and to the courts of the King.

Past the blue-sky of Earth's atmosphere... outside the blackness of outer space... and beyond the second heaven—

where the fallen angels dwell, lays the dominion and Kingdom of God—the third Heaven. It is a place where time and space does not exist. It is the dwelling place of the Most High God, and home to all that call upon the name of the Lord. It is the endless domain of Seraphim, Cherubim, Archangels, Light Bearers, and the Angelic Host of Heaven. Here, the plans of God are carried forth. And one-day, this kingdom will expand, and fill all, with the Glory of God. This kingdom is Nathan's home, and that is where he is headed.

He passed between the Twin Mountains of iron and soared across the Sea of Glass. Nathan flew on the currants of heaven, heading for a clearing at the foot of the Tree of Wisdom. The River of Life flowed alongside the tree. Its sole purpose: the healing of the nations and the gift of life. Nathan glanced up at the Courts of the King. Tall pillars of pure white marble, alongside smaller pillars of white fire that had at its core, cool blue flowing water, outlined the courtyard that led up to the Corridors of Truth.

Nathan made his way across the bridge that connected the forests of God with the Kingdom Proper. As he approached the Cherub stationed in front of the courts, Gabriel greeted him, "Our King is with you, my friend."

"Also with you, my brother." Nathan gave Gabriel a heartfelt embrace.

"The Council Chambers will surly heat-up today. The fallen-one has entered the Chamber Hall. He is more than ready to accuse us, and complain about our involvement in the life of John, and his mother. Come Nathan, we must take our place before the King. He has summoned us into His presence."

"The war continues Gabriel.... That fallen Cherub will never learn! Yet, in the core of his being, there is no light, and to his end, he will never partake in truth."

"Yes my brother, our Father has determined the end of all things. The time for revealing the Sons of God is approaching. Come, let us go." Gabriel and Nathan made their way to the upper halls, and down the corridor leading to the Chambers of the Most High.

Together, they passed through the Chamber of Worship and the Chamber of Incense, entering the tall golden gates that led to the Court of Judgment. The hall was full of Angelic Hosts lining the stadium seats overlooking the Hovering Throne of the Almighty. With heads bowed, and wings pointed back, they merged their voices in Angelic harmony. In perfect crescendo, they sang out the melody of the Lord—a single word... "Holy, Holy, Holy...." Not only was the chamber filled with this celestial sound but also the entirety of Heaven.

The Throne of God entered the great hall. The room was brilliant with the light and color of His Glory. A mosaic of brilliant glowing jewels and stones patterned the platform of His presence. Throughout the court, Light Bearers kneeled, illuminating His majesty. Four Seraphim, stationed at each corner of His Throne, reflected His image. Around the Throne, a massive silver rainbow filled the skies of eternity, glowing and mirroring all the colors of creation.

Gabriel and Nathan took their position in front of the chamber hall, kneeled next to the Seats of the Counsel, and sang out, "Holy... Holy... Holy..." In a moment of perfect sequence and unity, complete silence fell... not only in the chamber, but also throughout the third Heaven. The silence continued, until every creature in Heaven absorbed the Glory, Spirit, and Mind of Christ—every creature except two.

One was Satan, the fallen Cherub who once reflected the Master's glory and radiated His splendor in symphonic sound. He once was called the Anointed Cherub, but now he is known as Lucifer, the Prince of Darkness. He stood on the Platform of Petition. His gray appearance grew darker as his countenance filled with anger and disgust. The only place for him in Heaven was the Platform of Petition. Here, he is permitted to make his case, which consisted of accusations against the brethren and the Holy Angels. Day after day, he hurls his complaints, accusing humanity of every atrocity and challenging the grace and mercy of the Almighty. And, day after day he is confronted with the Scepter of Redemption. As a dog returning to its vomit, time after time, he crusades for the destruction of humanity, but in the end, he is left with only a few requests: "Let it be so." or "Silence!" from the King of all Kings and Lord of all Lords.

The second, a visitor whose spirit was brought forth from Earth to witness the decrees of the Lord, his heart was being made ready by the Spirit of the Most High to carry out His purpose and plan. Bo Jackson had been in a state of fasting and intersession for several days when the power of God caught him up to the Third Heaven.

Now, standing before the Alter of Incense, gazing at sights and listening to sounds, few humans have ever experienced, one of the Elders approached him saying, "Peace my brother, do not be afraid."

In an instant, all fear left his heart. Tears of joy filled his countenance. "What am I seeing?" he asked, puzzled by the proceedings before him.

"Bo, you've been brought here as a witness of the Lord. You will overhear the desires of His heart and know that our God is the God of gods, King of kings, and Lord of lords. Nothing is hidden before His eyes. All things are under the power of His wings. You will know, and in knowing, you will go forth and execute His will in this matter set before the tribunal this day."

The Elder reached out to the prophet and touched his forehead, releasing wisdom to understand the purpose of the Courts of the Lord. Clarity filled his mind. He had the knowledge that nothing happens in Heaven or on earth except through the Councils of the Almighty. He realized the power of the Alter of Incense and the prayers of the Saints. He gained insight regarding the interaction of the angelic and the affairs of humanity. Now, he was a witness to the accusations and powerlessness of the enemy and his unwilling submission to the Most High God.

Bo, amazed at the vastness of heaven's court, spanned the breadth of the Chamber, settling his eyes on the Platform of Petition. There, Satan stood, blanketed in a shroud of gray, reluctant to bow before the throne, but bow he must, for Holiness was present.

Satan lashed out and challenged the Lord and His wisdom, "Oh King, why do your warriors protect this woman? ...She is nothing! She is a blasphemer! ...How many times did she curse you? ...How many times did she deny your name?" In his belly, Satan's fury burned. His eyes grew red with evil and envy. He continued his oral assault, "How often did she desire to end her life? ...The life that you gave her! She no longer wants to live. She has rage in her heart ...and your Guardians keep protecting her. Why?" He was desperate, knowing that behind the scenes his minions were orchestrating her torment. "She does not deserve your protection.... She does not deserve your mercy!" Pride blinded him from understanding the meaning of redemption. In his twisted thinking, he thought he could even deceive the Most High God.

"SILENCE!" the voice of God echoed throughout the chamber. "ENOUGH! ...Be Still!" The words of the Most High thundered across the hall, shaking the pillars anchoring the Great Courts of the King.

Satan bowed with fear and trembling.

With brilliance, the light of God's glory began to fill and magnify the entirety of His Throne. When, out of the midst of the Throne, between the radiant white-light, a man arose.... It was the Son of Man.... It was the Son of God... the Redeemer, in full glory... whose splendor cannot be described, whose majesty, words cannot explain.

Stepping forward, Jesus stretched out His arms. The palms of His scarred hands glowed with brilliance. All the creatures of heaven fell to their faces and cried out in perfect unity, "Holy, Holy, Holy," as the sweet fragrance of Christ filled the chamber. All in the chamber rose to their feet. Lifting up their heads, they took in the breath of Him who sits on the throne. On cue, the Hosts of Heaven bowed. Silence fell across the Chamber of the Lord.... Satan wrapped his mangled wings around his face and hid from Him who lives forever and ever. All eyes shifted and were on him. The strange and heavy silence continued.

Jesus lowered His hands and reached for the Scepter of Redemption, strapped to His thigh. He held it up and pounded the floor three times, "Boom, Boom, Boom!" With a voice as strong as a thousand thunders, he spoke, "She is my child. Her debt has been paid!" At that moment, Satan vanished from the Tribunal hall. All the Hosts of Heaven raised their wings in jubilation and sang the song of the Lamb.

The Elder stood from his prone position and turned to help Bo to his feet. "Do you understand Bo?"

"Yes, I think I do." Bo answered with caution, knees still trembling from the awesome display of God's power.

"Go now. Think on these things. Soon, you will be told what you must do. Remember, think on these things— KNOW, our King is with you!"

6 THE DREAM

o woke, not to the sound of the Sophar, but to
the blaring sound of a trumpet through his bedroom window. Its ear-piercing melody, floated up
from his next-door neighbor's house. Timmy O'Brian prac-
ticed for band every day. When he did, it not only blew
the pictures off his parent's wall, but also woke everyone
in a two-block radius. Fortunate for Bo, he lived next
door, and the screech of missed notes threw him out of
bed—skipping the stage of tossing and turning with a pillow wrapped around his face and ears.

His first thought: "*I'm back.*" He felt as if he returned
from another dimension—thrust out of the heavens and

crashing into his bedroom. *"A difficult feat for the most able-bodied, but someone my age: remarkable,"* he thought. The trance like dream was still alive in his mind. The thought of his experience hit him, shaking him back to reality.

The sound of Timmy's trumpet went silent. Bo got up off the floor and started his morning ritual: talking to God, aloud, and direct. "Wow, Father, now that's a journey!" mumbling to God, as he made his way downstairs to make a pot of coffee.

Wiping sleep from his eyes, he reached for that old percolator he loved so much. "Now what Papa?" he said lifting his eyes to heaven, "I'm ready.... Let's get this show on the road!" With fire and zeal, he was ready to take on this mission of the Lord.

God loved that about this old prophet. He was direct, bold, eager, and above all, seasoned. He learned through the rough roads of life, "how" to listen and "when" to move. God had taught him, "what" to say and "when" to be silent, "when" to pray and "when" to blaze in with fiery anointing.

To some, Bo appeared to be a stubborn old man. In fact, he is a simple straight shooter, with little tolerance for psychobabble opinions, when someone needs to be set free. He is a seasoned prophet who, at the command of God, could read your mail quicker than a dishonest postal worker. When he calls for the power of God, God shows up and folks are healed and delivered.

This experience troubled Bo, he thought, "*Why did he choose me? Why was I taken to the Council Chambers? Papa, why was I there? What do you want me to do?*" His questions kept rolling out of his mouth. He had witnessed the Redeemer rebuking Satan with thunderous splendor.

God just listened, as this old man recycled his thinking.

"*What did the Elder mean? 'Think on these things.' What did he mean? 'KNOW the King is with you.'*" Confused, Bo asked, "Lord, you know me... I know you're with me Lord. Did I do something wrong?" His countenance dropped as he wrestled with his own humanity. "Did I disappoint you Lord?"

"Oh be quiet, you old fool," the Lord responded with comforting jest.

Bo laughed. "Yes Lord..." he said with a reluctant grin on his face, "I love you Lord!"

"I love you too... now listen up!"

"Yes Lord," Bo said. His head was tucked downward with a slight crooked smile on his face.

"This time tomorrow, I will show you where to go. Once there, I will tell you what to do. For now, write down the things you have seen, and think on those things. When the time comes, you will be equipped to act—to run the race I have set before you."

"Yes Lord."

"Do you understand?"

"Yes Lord."

Bo wanted to enter this battle—this is his life, he lives and walks in this reality. It is too bad few Christians understand this reality. Bo grabbed his cup of coffee and headed for his study to write in his journal.

South of Pelican Bay, Aunt Chloe heard the voice of Jasmine calling out for her upstairs, "Aunt Chloe ... Aunt Chloe ... Come here... Please come here." Chloe was Jasmine's guardian. She raised her since she was a toddler.

Chloe rushed upstairs to see if Jasmine was okay. Chloe always had a watchful eye on her. There she was, still in bed with her covers pulled up to her head. "Are you alright sweetie?"

"Yes Ma'am, I just wanted to talk for a second."

"What's up baby?"

"Would you pray with me?" Jasmine asked with a soft-spoken whisper.

"Sure sweetie. Did your nightmares come back?"

"No Aunt Chloe. They've been gone for a long time. I think someone needs my help."

"What do you mean Jasmine?"

"Well... I dreamt about a lady in the hospital with her eyes closed, and... I think I'm supposed to pray for her."

"Ok Baby, we better get with it and do some praying. Is she a friend of yours?"

"No, I saw her in my dream. She needs our prayers."

Jasmine was glad Aunt Chloe didn't think she was strange. About a year ago, Jasmine came close to getting shot in a store robbery. If it weren't for the brave sacrifice of a complete stranger, Jasmine would have been killed. His name was Todd Parker. He jumped in front of her, shielding her from the bullet. This stranger saved Jasmine's life, but in the process, he was killed. Not a day goes by, that Jasmine does not give thanks to God, for what that man did. It was hard at first. For months, she had nightmares. Then she said, "One day, God just took all my pain away." She has had a close relationship with Him ever since. So when Jasmine tells her Aunt she needs to pray, Chloe jumps right in, no questions asked.

Now, she prays for complete strangers. "Ok Jasmine. Let's pray." Chloe took hold of Jasmine's hand and together they ushered up prayers to heaven, asking Jesus to intervene and help this dear lady in all her pain.

They prayed together for quite a while until Jasmine looked up and said, "She's going to be okay now, Aunt Chloe. Jesus told me He had it all under control."

Yet, unknown to either Jasmine or Aunt Chloe, the woman she saw in her dream was Sara, the wife of Todd

Parker, the man who saved Jasmine's life. Sara was lying in a hospital bed, in a coma.

7 LIVE

Sheriff Philip Rosen, a rugged third generation cop who grew-up on New York's Upper East Side, had a nose for sniffing out difficult cases: he had seen everything. Working the streets of NY had toughened his senses, but this one had him baffled. *"What's wrong with me?"* he thought. *"Where's my edge? Come on Phil—get it together!"*

He stared through the window of Sara's hospital room, transfixed by her motionless body bound with hoses, wires, and monitors. Drawn to the quietness of her spirit, questions flooded his mind, *"Where did she come from? Why was she lying on the road like that? How did she get out of the car?"* This thought troubled him, *"The medics said she had a baby, where the heck is it? What is going on here?"*

The last two years in Florida had been more than a vacation—hibernation. He was running... hiding... but from what? He didn't know himself. Now, that cop's intuition started to kick-in. He hated his job In NY; started drinking; became fatigued and withdrawn. Sleep? Barely. Nightmares kept him awake most nights. The only comfort he found came from a bottle of Crown and the solitude he had in his own self-pity. He thought, *"I don't mind the work... small town in Florida... way better than NY! I was killing myself up there."* For Phil, anything is better than becoming a drunken NY detective on the verge of self-destruction.

The only exhilaration he found on the job, these days, consisted of writing too many tickets and chasing down too many teenagers. He stared down at Sara's lifeless body—at the mystery surrounding this helpless woman. *"I need to go back to the scene. Wait... Crime scene! Is it a crime?"* He asked himself, *"Maybe I'll find a clue?"*

Nikita ran a soft cotton washcloth across baby John's face, around his eyes, and down his cheeks. She admired the smallness of his hands and the softness of his skin. "What's up with you little John? What does God have in store for you?" She took hold of his tiny hand with her finger, leaned over brushing his cheek with her nose, and whispered, "You're a special one little child. You are a very special one!" She washed around his mouth and under his chin. "So little... You are such a tiny little man." With care, she leaned his body forward, embracing his neck with her palm, and began washing his back, when she noticed something. "What? Oh my, what happened here?" She mumbled to herself. "Danny, check this out," pointing to the back of baby John's neck, "Is it a bruise?"

Leaning over Nikita, Danny stared at a large mark on baby John's neck. "It must be a birthmark?"

Nikita traced the outline with her finger. "It looks like a lightning bolt." That's what it was, a heavenly honed bolt of lightning extended across the full length of his neck and down the center of his back.

"That's a strange birthmark... looks more like a tattoo." Danny had his own share of tattoos; the detail of this birthmark was definitely artistic.

Nikita dried off the baby and dressed him in one of her t-shirts. She sat in a chair next to the bed and gave him a bottle, rocking him to sleep. As she rocked, she whispered a sweet melody in his ear, "*Jesus loves you, this I know... for the Bible tells me so... little ones, to Him belong... they are weak, but He is strong. Yes, Jesus loves you....*" Little John fell asleep, with a bottle hanging from the edge of his lips. Nikita's face rested on top of his head in a warm cuddle. She wondered about his mother. "*Lord, give me wisdom—don't let my heart get too attached to this little guy.*" The baby captured Nikita's heart, but she realized they were only guardians for the Lord. Nikita whispered into his ear, "*You need your mother; don't you little John.*"

It's been two weeks since Bo's third Heaven experience. Growing restless he prayed, "Lord, have I missed it somehow? I'm trying to understand." The response was silence. Bo recognized the meaning of silence—it's a flag post, a stop sign, a point of waiting, a place where patience kicks into gear and all that's left is to pray. Bo went upstairs to get dressed. Sitting on the edge of his bed, he started praying again, "I call on you Father. I lift-up your Holy name. I seek your face this day. Father, bring forth your will in this situation, send your angels Lord, and cause your word to manifest—here... now... on earth as it is in heaven!"

Before he finished praying a light as bright as the noonday filled his room. Nathan, a glorious Heavenly warrior, manifested his presence and was towering over him.

Bo, overcome by the messenger's brilliance, fell to his knees, trembling at the awesomeness of the angel's stature.

"Be at peace, Bo.... Do not be afraid, the King is with you!" Nathan sensing his fear, reached out and touched the top of Bo's head, saying, "Fear not oh servant of the Most High God! Receive the peace of the Lord! My name is Nathan, Captain of the Lord's host. I come to you with a message from the Most High."

Like a current of electricity, a wave of peace moved through Bo's entire body, causing every nerve to tingle. His breathing became heavy, his eyelids started to flutter, and his lips stammered. Speechless, he stood to his feet. With his head still bowed in awe he stuttered, "What must I do?"

"Lift your head Bo, like you; I am a servant of God. The Lord knows your prayers.... From the moment you set your face to understand what His will is in this matter, he sent me to you. The forces of darkness hindered my arrival. For two weeks, I battled against the Prince and Power of the air. Michael, a Mighty Archangel who stands in defense of the Lord's people, came to my aid. At last, I am here to tell you what you must do in this hour." His voice penetrated Bo's soul.

Bo nodded in agreement, still unable to express himself.

"Arise Bo and go to Florida, to the town of Perry. You will be shown what to do, when you arrive." Then Nathan vanished out of his sight.

Bo stood, bewildered by the experience. His body still tingled from the presence of the angel. He kneeled and began to cry out in desperate prayer, "Papa, I praise your name. I worship you, Lord God Almighty.... I seek your face, and submit to your will. Please protect me, give me wisdom. Cover me under the shelter of your wings. Light my path, and guide my steps. Give me strength, and discernment. Let your Kingdom come! Let your will be done! In the blessed name of Jesus, I pray."

Bo sat in silence waiting on God for a conformation in his spirit. He sensed the presence of angels in the past, but never like this. Bo believed that God often sends His angels, to execute His plans and desires for His saints. Throughout the scriptures, angelic visitations are commonplace, especially during times when God is moving powerfully amongst the affairs of men. He needed to be sure. The scriptures state to test all things. For Bo, prayer was his first line of defense.

As Bo sat before the Lord he felt the presence of the Holy Spirit come upon him and the voice of God spoke to Him, "Go Bo. Go to the place I have called you to!"

Bo smiled, got to his feet and started to prepare for his trip. In his mind, he rehearsed the events witnessed in his heavenly vision. He wondered about Sara, "*Why was the enemy so desperate to get her?*"

Philip returned from the crime scene baffled... "Not a shred of evidence, not a hint of a clue. Dead-ends, everywhere I turn... dead-ends; now what do I do? If she would only wake up... God, I could use your help." Phil wasn't a religious man. The only time he spoke to God was in vain, or in anger, but he was getting desperate. He interviewed Henry and Barbara Stevens, the family that called 911, and came up with nothing. Their story was a little inconsistent; they were heading north on vacation, but were driving south when they came across the accident. Henry said it was God that brought them there. Barbara said angels were watching over her. One thing they all agreed on: she would have died if they hadn't happened upon the scene.

Bo arrived in Tallahassee a little after 2:00 PM. He rented a car and headed to Perry. Not knowing what to expect, he prayed for guidance, and then he thought, *"Now this is what I call... moving out in faith."* He was thinking of Abraham, how God called him out of Haran, to the Land of Canaan, but didn't know where, or why, he was going— Abraham moved in faith, because he believed God. Bo felt the same way.

About half way there, Bo turned into a service station. He stood at the back of the car pumping gas. A homeless man approached him, stuttering, "Sir, na-na-need your w-wa...windows washed?"

"Well, sure friend, go ahead." Bo gave him a nod and a smile. After he paid the attendant, he went inside to use the restroom. When he came out, the man was sitting in the front seat. "Hey! What are you doing in my car?"

"Sir, I ne-ne-need a ride u-up the road, c-ca-can you p-pa-please give me a ride?"

The man seemed sincere. "How far are you going? Bo asked."

"I ne-need to get to Pe-Perry, its' a-a-about an hour fr-from here. My sick fr-friend … in the hospital."

"Perry, hum. It so happens, I'm headed that way."

"So, ca-an I ride wi-with you?"

"Sure, not a problem." Bo didn't believe in coincidence—the hand of God orchestrates all things.

Overjoyed, the homeless man said, "Tha- thank you… God ble-bless you sir."

Bo went back in the store and bought a couple of sodas, two sandwiches, and a couple bags of chips. "*He must be hungry,*" he thought. Bo handed him the food, then sat back, with watered eyes, watching him eat his sandwich.

Back at the hospital, Phil bumped into Doctor Bloom. "Hey Doc, what's the status on our Jane Doe?"

"Still unconscious Sheriff; trauma to the brain. We haven't isolated it. No swelling to speak of, and that's good news. And her eyes… well, let's say responsive. Ribs are healing well. Have you had any replies from the ad you placed in the paper?"

"Not a word, she's like a ghost. We did a background check on her prints and came up dry. I called in the CI unit from Tallahassee, hoping they could come up with something... anything, but nothing. This is a real mystery Doc."

"Too bad Sheriff. You understand we are a small hospital. We should think about sending her to the city. I am not sure how long we can sustain her."

"Give me a few more days. I need to find out who she is."

"I have a staff meeting tomorrow, we will discuss it, but I need to think about what's best for the patient."

"I understand. Do you mind if I sit with her for a while?"

"Go ahead Sheriff."

Philip needed some quiet time, a place to gather his thoughts. He could think of no better place, than by Sara's side.

Bo had a peaceful ride to Perry. His newfound friend didn't talk much. He asked, "What's your name friend?"

"Na-than, my name is Na-Nathan." As they approached Perry, Nathan said to Bo, "Pa-please, ne-next off ramp, if you do-do-don't mind, ta-turn right."

"Sure, I'll take you all the way. If it's ok with you, I'd like to pray for you and your friend?"

"Su-sure," he replied, "I'd li-like that."

They maneuvered through the small town of Perry, following the signs to the Hospital, making their way to the parking area in front of the ER. As Bo parked the car and was getting out, Nathan gazed at Bo for a moment, and said (without a stutter), *"Know that the King is with you!"*

"What did you say?" but no Nathan; he disappeared out of his sight. Bo looked around the parking lot and towards the entrance to the hospital, "Nathan? Nathan?" nothing, silence, the man had vanished. Bo remembered that scripture in the book of Hebrews (13:2), *"Do not forget to entertain strangers, for by so doing some people have entertained angels without knowing it."*

Bo leaned his head across the top of the car, closed his eyes, and started to pray, when that all too familiar, small still voice, returned, "She's in there.... Sara's in the hospital."

Cayla stood with a team of angels stationed on top of the roof. Nathan shot up through the heavens. Cayla went and told Raphael, "The Prophet is here."

"Good," Raphael replied, "Go back to your post until they leave. Send one of your Scouts to the Intercessors house and prepare them for Sara's arrival."

"Yes sir," Cayla said, and then passed through the ceiling to his position on the roof.

Philip sat next to Sara, holding her hand, as he mumbled a simple prayer. Without warning, her blood pressure rapidly dropped, sounding off monitors and alarms, everywhere. Two nurses ran into the room to check her machine. "What's happening? What's going on?" Phil panicked.

"Call Doctor Bloom, code red, room 33—Hurry." Then she turned to Phil and said, "Sorry Sheriff, you need to leave."

Phil watched through the window until the nurse closed the curtain. Another nurse ran in pushing a Defibrillator through the door.

Doctor Bloom burst through door at the end of the corridor, glancing at the Sheriff as he entered her room. It was chaos everywhere. They worked on Sara for several minutes, trying to get her heart to start.... "Clear!" nothing. Again, "Clear," still flat. Again, "CLEAR," no movement at all, still in defib. He handed the paddles to the nurse, and then began to pound on her chest... again, and again, but no response. "I don't understand this.... What happened?" Then Doctor Bloom called it, "She's gone, 3:33 PM." Confused, he turned aside, head down, and walked out the door.

Shocked, Phil said, "Doc, what's going on? Doctor, please?"

Doctor Bloom approached him, upset "I don't... I don't understand what happened. She's gone sheriff."

"What?"

"She's gone. I'm sorry, her heart gave out."

"How? What happened? You said she was doing well."

"I don't know Sheriff!"

"How can this be? What's going on around here?" Phil broke down and started to cry.

Doctor Bloom placed his arm around him and motioned to the nurse to bring over a chair. "Please sit down, Sheriff."

"This doesn't make any sense. Let me be!" He sat down weeping. Phil wasn't one to show emotions, he was a rock and never had time for tears. He felt broken, his nerves shot; this woman, this case, awakened his soul. He cried out, "Why God? Why?"

Moments later, Bo pushed open the doors at the end of the hall. Looking at a nurse standing in the corridor he asked in a loud voice, "Where's Sara's room?" No one responded. As he walked towards the nurse's station, he started feeling an incredible surge of the Lord's presence.

"Excuse me, nurse, please tell me, where's Sara's room? ...I know she's here... mid-thirties... auburn hair and...."

Sheriff Rosen stood to his feet and interrupted Bo, "Nurse, it's our Jane Doe." Phil was certain of it.

Bo turned and asked, "Jane Doe? Where is she?"

The nurse called out to Doctor Bloom, "Doctor, you better get over here. Sir, please have a seat the Doctor will be right with you."

"I don't need to sit! I need to see Sara."

Phil placed his hand on Bo's shoulder and asked, "Her name is Sara?"

"Yes, Sara!"

"Are you a relative?" asked the nurse.

Bo turned to where the Sheriff was sitting and started heading for her room behind him.

The nurse called out, "Wait. Sir, you can't go in there."

Bo didn't listen. He just kept walking.

"Sheriff, I don't think..."

"I'll take care of it." Phil reached for Bo and touched his shoulder.

Bo turned and said, "This is for the Glory of God. Now stand back, please. Let me see her."

The sheriff stopped in his tracks.

The Doctor ran over, but Phil reached out and stopped him, "Let him be."

They both stood there watching from the door as Bo walked into the room. He folded back the sheet that covered her head. When he saw her, tears of joy filled his eyes; he remembered Sara and Todd from the conference— he remembered the prophecy concerning her baby. "Sara, it's you...." He lifted his head to heaven, raised his arms up, and started praising God.

The presence of the Lord filled the room. Phil couldn't move. He froze, overcome by the wave of God's presence sweeping over him.

"Father, I praise you that all life and breath is in your hands, I ask you to send your power and move on Sara. Breathe your life into her spirit and cause her to live and not die." Joy rose up inside Bo. His hands became hot like fire. He reached down, placed them on Sara's cheeks, and said, "Send your Holy Spirit; Lord, send your angels."

Unknown to all standing, Raphael and his team of angels were positioned around the bed with heads bowed and wings outstretched in a protective shield around the room.

The presence of the Lord intensified. Bo said, "*Show them your glory, Lord.*"

While they all peered into the room, it became as bright as noonday. Angels stood around Sara with their heads bowed. A holy melody filled the air.

Doctor Bloom was in awe. "What am I seeing?"

A nurse whispered, "It's the glory of God."

Bo, filled with the Holy Spirit, said, *"Now child, rise, and see the salvation of the Lord. In the name of Jesus, I say, arise."*

At that moment, her body began to convulse. She gulped and gasped for air. "She is alive," said Bo, "The Lord has raised her from the dead."

Everyone in the room fell to their knees. They were all filled with the glory of God.

The light vanished and the angels disappeared out of their sight.

Raphael said to one of his Scouts, "Report to Nathan what has happened. We are on the move."

"Yes sir," said the Scout, "I just love to see the glory of God."

"I know my friend.... He is glorious. Now, make haste. The King is with you."

"Also with you my friend," then he looked up to heaven, pointed his wings upward, and shot through the ceiling, into the heavens.

Bo turned towards Sara, "Sara, it's me... Bo."

Sara wrapped her arms around him, still reeling from the presence of God. "The Lord is so good, so good and mighty... Where am I? How did you get here?"

"It's ok Sara; take it easy, you need nourishment."

Peace flowed over her in waves.

Sheriff Rosen walked in and stood next to Bo. "Please, I don't understand what just happened; I need the Lord, please help me."

Bo looked at Phil and said, "This day is the day of your salvation. The Lord has blessed you, and permitted you to witness His glory. Now, be empowered and receive the gift of His salvation." He placed his hand on Phil's shoulder and prayed, "Lord, this child of yours, comes to you now, in the name of your son Jesus. He knows that he is a sinner and seeks your forgiveness. He wants to be born again, in your kingdom. Holy Spirit come... fill him with your presence."

Before Bo could finish praying, Philip started shaking from the power of the Spirit. With stammered lips, he cried out, "*Thank you Lord.*" Tears of joy poured out from him, but not him alone. Behind Phil, the entire nursing staff was on the floor with their faces to the ground, thanking God for their own salvation. Doctor Bloom praised God, and started speaking melodies in an unknown language.

Sara lay there, beaming with the glow of God's presence. Sheriff Rosen rested his arm on Sara's bed. Tears of salvation filled his eyes. There she was, alive again.

8 JOHN

Nikita peeked in to check on the baby, he was still
asleep. She walked down the hallway to the
kitchen, grabbed her cup of unfinished coffee, and
placed it in the microwave. "Shoot, what a wasted day, I
need to pray." For years, Nikita interceded in prayer. Every morning, like clockwork, she would get up and bow her
head to seek guidance from the Lord and lift up friends
and family in prayer.

She reached for the paper, bowed her head, and prayed,
"Father, I'm sorry for not seeking you today. What's
wrong with me? Lord, please—bless the rest of my day.
God open my eyes and ears. Help me to understand your

will. Guide my thoughts.... Bless baby John. Bring his mother to him safely. Father, wherever she is, pour out your blessings. Protect this household. Send your angels."

She continued as she read the paper, "Father, show me your burdens...." Nikita prayed for the nation, Ronald and Nancy Reagan and the hostage crisis. "Give him wisdom in dealing with Iran and Iraq. Give him insight and strength him as he moves against the Soviet aggression in Afghanistan," she paused, and bowed a second time trying to listen to the Spirit... but He seemed quiet.

Nikita stopped, searching for burdens to lift up to heaven. She hummed praises to God as she read, but her song soon became a song of war, a cry to the Most High to intervene.

A WOMAN IS SLAIN, A SHERIFF CONFESSES

TAMPA—Red lights flashed behind the woman's car. She wondered why she was being stopped. The Plant City woman pulled her blue Honda Accord to the side of the road near Highway 41. She was never seen alive again.

"What's happening in this world? Jesus, please be with her family and her children. God, give them peace. Pour out your Spirit and let justice reign. Lord—be in this situation." Nikita read further as her heart got closer to God.

MIDEAST TURMOIL—DYLAN URGES ISRA-EL TO SEEK PEACE TALKS

JERUSALEM—Senate Democratic leader Robert Dylan urged Israel to move towards peace… "We encouraged everybody to sit around the table and start having dialogue. Children are dying the killing must STOP."

Over and over she read, praying and sending petitions to the Lord. The bold-faced type was jumping out at her as she read the headlines aloud to herself.

BLOOD BATH IN SOUTH AFRICA, 87 LAY DEAD

SERIAL KILLER LOOSE IN N.Y.

KIDDIE PORN CASE GOES TO TRIAL

ABORTION FOES JAILED—OUTBREAK AT D.C. RALLY

"Dear God, where do I begin? Hear my cries God, see my tears."

TEACHER SUSPENDED—TEN COMMAND-MENTS NOT ALLOWED IN SCHOOL

U.F.O. FEVER HITS BELGIUM

"Jesus, pour out your Spirit. Bring revival to the land. Send us out, dear God. Send us out, the harvest is ripe for your touch—rain down on us God—we need your sweet rain."

Nikita's eyes were opened to the era in which she lived. She couldn't believe what she was reading. Line after line the signs of the times spoke to her spirit.

She closed her eyes and rested her head on the paper, her face cupped in the palms of her hands, praying silently. The words flowed as the Spirit gave her utterance.

She opened her eyes and glanced down at the corner of the paper, and read.

JANE DOE SURVIVES ACCIDENT—LOSSES IDENTITY

PERRY—On July 11 at 3:00 AM, forty miles south of I-10, a car spun out of control and burst into flames. Barbara and Henry Stone were first on the scene. They were heading down the highway on vacation, when they saw flames illuminating the night sky in front of them. As they approached the area, they discovered the source of the flames—a car exploded and was on fire. On the side of the road, they found a woman, lying in the dirt, unconscious.

Sheriff Rosen, of Perry, stated she was pregnant, and apparently gave birth at the scene. No child was found. "The woman was definitely pregnant." Sheriff Rosen stated, "Where's the baby? We found nothing."

The woman, "Jane Doe," had no identification. There was no evidence indicating, who she was, where she came from, or the whereabouts of her baby. Jane Doe is in a comma. Authorities are asking for your help. If anyone has information regarding this accident, or the missing child, please contact the Perry Sheriff's Office at this toll-free number, 1-800-555-1211.

As Nikita read, the Spirit of God rested on her. Her hands began to tremble, and a deep surge of the Spirit filled her heart. Uncontrollably, she cried and prayed, tears running down her face and onto the paper. She felt the burden of the Lord—His heart towards this woman. She prayed with earnest commission.

In the midst of her prayer, a small still voice filtered through her thoughts, *"This is John's mother."*

"Oh my God... Father—this is John's mother?" Chills ran down her neck and arms, "Lord, what should I do?"

An angel stood behind Nikita and whispered into her mind, "*Call Sheriff Rosen, speak only to him.*"

The buzz of Sara's incredible recovery was moving through the hospital like a whirlwind. By lunch, hospital employees gathered on Sara's floor, in hopes to get a glimpse of the woman, and her miracle.

Doctor Bloom, still in a daze over the events, had to bring order to the floor. After meeting with the hospital administrator, he called his team over and directed them to clear the area, "We need to secure this wing. In spite of what happened, we have a job to do. No one, not authorized to be here, must leave. I am suspending visitor's hours till 2:00 PM."

Phil was sound asleep. He hadn't slept that peaceful in years. He dreamt about Sara and her baby; she was holding her baby in front of a pier, watching the sunrise. Behind her was an enormous pelican. Sara was glowing with maternal affection. The sky filled with brilliant shades of orange and red....

A nurse shook his arm, trying to wake him, "Sheriff, you have a phone call."

Startled, Phil opened his eyes, "What... oh, sorry, sleepy I guess."

"Sheriff, the phone—it's for you. She said it was important."

"OK, I'll be right there." He rolled off the cot and stared at Sara for a second, thinking about his dream. Sara was sound asleep.

He made his way to the nurse's station and reached for the phone, "Sheriff Rosen, can I help you?"

"Sheriff, its Alice.... There is a woman on hold. She says she must speak to you. It's about your Jane Doe."

There was a moment of silence on the phone. Hesitantly, Nikita spoke up, "Hello Sheriff, my name is Nikita Bean. I have information regarding the woman in the paper, and her baby."

Phil's ears perked up, "Yes, go ahead."

"Well Sheriff, you're not going to believe this...." Nikita was not sure how to tell him, "I believe we have the baby."

"Hold on... what do you mean, you have the baby?"

"Yes Sheriff," Nikita was getting nervous.

"Mrs. Bean, where are you?"

"Sheriff, the baby was left with us... to care for until his mother..."

Phil interrupted her... "Ma'am, where are you?" Philip was starting to get edgy. "What makes you think that this is the missing child?"

"Sheriff, please, let me explain. My husband and I live in Pelican Bay and we..."

The Sheriff cut in again. "Did you say, Pelican Bay?"

"Yes Sheriff.... My husband Danny had a dream and we started praying, and, well, while we were praying, I had a vision of an angel coming to our house. He had a baby in his arms.... I know it's hard to believe—but it's true. Honest."

Phil sensed, God orchestrating this call. As soon as he heard Pelican Bay—it hit him, he thought, "*My dream, the pier, the Pelican, this must be God.*" He continued, "No, go ahead Ma'am, it's alright; you were saying you had a vision—about an angel?"

"Yes. God told us we would hear a knock at the door, and when we opened it, we would find a baby. He even told us the baby's name. His name is John. It is, isn't it?"

"Nikita, let me ask you something: Do you live by a pier?"

"Sure do. We live right on the bay, Pelican Bay. Do you know the place?" She was feeling a bit more comfortable.

"I sure do, been there on vacation a couple times. It's on Santa Maria Key, about 350 miles south from here. Ma'am, can I please get your number?"

Nikita gave him her phone number and address, and then asked him a question, "Is she baby John's mother?"

"I think she just might be. Let me call you back in a few minutes."

Nikita hung up the phone, still a little shaky over the conversation. *"Oh my God,"* she thought, *"He probably thinks I'm a nutcase."*

Phil taken aback by the conversion, stood with a blank expression on his face, hand still on the receiver, *"Hope this is real—sure don't want to get her hopes up."* Phil walked back to Sara's room. She was still sleeping. He softly shook her shoulder, "Sara, I need to ask you something."

Sheepishly, Sara opened her eyes, "Hi Sheriff...."

"Please Sara, call me Phil."

"Ok... Phil," She said.

"What's your baby's name?"

Sara started to tear up, "We wanted to call him John.... Why do you ask?"

Phil couldn't believe his ears. His hair now standing on end, he replied with a big smile, "I just can't believe this... this whole thing is so crazy.... I think I found your baby."

"What did you say?" Sara wrapped her arms around Phil, "Oh my God, are you kidding? Thank you... thank you! Is he ok? Where is he? Oh thank you Lord, thank you Lord."

Phil told Sara about his dream, that strange phone call, the pelican, the pier, the baby's name, and about Nikita and her vision. "Sara, when you said 'John,' I knew for sure!" He called Nikita back and got directions to her house.

Phil walked over to wake Bo, "Good news Bo. We found Sara's baby." Phil could hardly contain himself. "Come on old timer, we gotta get movin."

"Shoot! I wish I could go with you. I haven't had this much fun, in, well... I can't remember when...."

"You're not going?" Sara interrupted.

"No darling, my work is done here, and the Lord wants me back in Kansas."

"Oh Bo, thank you so much." Sara wiped a tear from her eye, reached out and embraced him.

"Its okay sweetie, my prayers are always with you and your child. I'm a phone-call away. The Lord knitted you to my heart—forever. Take care of your baby Sara. Remember the Prophecy; *know that the King is with you!*"

Bo turned to Phil; he was hiding his emotions, "Sheriff, you now have a new life in Christ. Walk it out in humility and seek His face daily. Read your bible, and call me anytime, I mean anytime! You're a good man Sheriff; the Lord loves you very much."

Speechless, all Phil could say was, "Thank you, thank you so much Bo! You gave me my life back, and Sara... I don't know what to say!"

"No my son, He gave you your life back," pointing to heaven with a giant smile on his face. Then he grabbed a hold of Phil and gave him a big bear hug. Turning away he said, "Remember—Know the King is with you!" and he walked out of the room. Sara and Phil just stood there in wonderment.

Doctor Bloom walked in and said, "How's my miracle girl doing?"

"Doc," Phil said, "We need to get out of here. We found Sara's baby. It's a long story. I'll tell you all about it when I get back from Pelican Bay."

"Yes Doctor, thank you so much," Sara said, and gave him a hug and a kiss on the cheek, "You will always be in my heart."

After saying their goodbyes to the nursing staff, Sara and Phil started their five-hour drive to Pelican Bay.

9 TOGETHER

The ride over to Pelican Bay went by quickly. Phil and Sara talked like long lost friends—they were bonding. The events over the last few weeks left Phil raw, and emotional. Sitting next to Sara, in route to pick up her baby, was more than he could have imagined a week ago. He caught himself staring, and then quickly turned away, when she glanced back in his direction. He thought, "*I feel like a love-sick teenager.*"

Sara stared down at her lap, smiling. In those uncomfortable silent moments, she wondered, "*Who is this man? He's not so bad... somewhat good looking. He's so kind...*

seems to care." She said, "Phil, you think my baby's alright?" The thought of seeing her baby made her nervous.

"Don't worry Sara; I'm sure he's fine. If there's one thing I've learned this past week, it's like Bo said, the Lord is with us. Believe me Sara; I never thought those words would come out of my mouth, but it's as true as I'm sitting here with you. I believe that with all my heart!"

Sara smiled, "You're so right. God is good! His mercy endures forever." She sat back and thought about all the miracles God had done and how strange things had been.

Phil changed the topic, wanting to understand more about Sara, and the chain of events that started this journey, "You and Bo seemed to be friends."

"I met Bo at a conference with my husband shortly after we got married." She wasn't sure if she wanted to go down that road. She explained how they met. She talked about her past and her childhood. "I could never trust men until I met Todd." Sara started to tear up, "He was a Godly man... He saved my life."

Phil was going to ask what she meant by "was" but decided against it, and just listened.

"He led me to the Lord. He was my soul mate. We wanted kids from the start, but the doctors told me it wasn't possible." She paused for a second, rubbing her eyes. "When we met Bo, kids were the last thing on my mind. Sure enough, he prophesied we would have a son, he would be a great man of God, and be used mightily for the kingdom. I got pregnant, not long after." Sara started to cry.

"Are you ok?"

"I'm fine. It's so hard sometimes."

"Let's talk about something else." Phil said.

"No, I want to talk about it. It helps." In her mind, she wanted to get the emotions out, now, before they got to Pelican Bay. "The day I found out I was pregnant, my husband died in a terrible accident."

"I'm sorry," Phil was speechless.

"It's ok... gotta be strong; need to move on for Johnny's sake. He is my gift from God and he needs his mother." She shifted gears, "Phil, do you think he will recognize me? I mean he has never seen me."

"Sara... I believe he will. You carried him in the comfort of your womb for nine months."

Sara's mind was going a thousand miles an hour. "Where are we going to live? I left everything behind me when Todd passed."

"You are right where you're supposed to be for the moment. You're alive, your baby is safe, and we're on our way to get him." Phil wanted to be supportive, he understood "starting over," and now with God in the picture, it changes everything. "Take it one step at a time. First, we'll get your child. Everything else will fall into place, I assure you!"

"You're right... it's going to work out—everything else has. Besides, before the accident I was depressed. God will supply all my needs according to His riches and glory in heaven."

"Amen!" Phil answered with a smile.

"Amen, brother!" Now they were both laughing and thanking God for His incredible goodness.

They approached the I-75 turnoff to Pelican Bay.

Sara's union with her baby was as expected, a heartfelt event that touched everyone deeply. They met in front of the historic City Pier. Nikita was sitting on a bench feeding the baby. Danny was leaning against a handrail, staring out at the bay, watching a sailboat regatta, when he heard a voice behind him.

"Nikita.... Are you Nikita?" Phil was walking towards them.

Nikita stood up with a warm smile, "Sara?"

Sara said tearfully, "My baby... Johnny, you're so little...." She reached out and took hold of her child. "Thank you, thank you so much for taking care of him!" She kissed him, hugged him, and checked his toes, fingers, and little hands. Sara was ecstatic, "You're so beautiful." Baby

John smiled, holding tightly to Sara's finger. As if on cue, the bells at the Island Community Church began to ring. They rang every hour from 9:00 AM to 6:00 PM, first the time then an old gospel hymn, now the bells rang out "How Great Thou Art."

> *"O Lord my God, When I in awesome wonder,*
> *Consider all the worlds Thy Hands have made;*
> *I see the stars, I hear the rolling thunder,*
> *Thy power throughout the universe displayed."*

Danny and Phil stood there listening, as the sound of the bells framed the moment. It was an emotional meeting; everyone was crying and praising God. After hugs and introductions, Danny said, "I put together a barbeque.... Let's head back to the house. I'm sure everyone's hungry."

They all nodded in agreement and headed down Mangrove Avenue towards their house, Danny leading the way. "I hope you like dolphin fish—I'm cooking BBQ mahimahi with mango Salsa, BBQ shrimp—New Orleans style, grilled veggies, and coconut rice."

Phil's eyes lit up with hunger and excitement, "Now that's what I'm talking about!"

Sara laughed, hugging her baby. Nikita put her arm around her in a warm embrace, "Everything is going to be alright."

Nathan and Raphael were invisibly walking behind them when Nathan said to Raphael, "God is glorious my friend."

"Yes he is, Nathan—yes he is."

"The King has requested that you be stationed with this family. Stay with them and guard their every step. This is a house of prayer and the enemy is fearful to approach, but he is extremely cunning. There is one word for this job—protection—that is your number one objective. Do you understand?"

"Yes Nathan. Understood!"

"Take Cayla with you. He can watch over Phil, he is new to the Kingdom."

"We got this Nathan."

"The Sophar has sounded. I'm being summoned. I will see you when I return. The King is with you."

"Also with you, God's speed!"

Nathan lifted his wings and spun through the clouds into the heavens. Raphael called Cayla and they hustled off to the barbeque, observing from a branch on a nearby magnolia tree.

During their time together, they discussed many things. Nikita and Sara were bonding quickly. To Sara's surprise, the open hearts of Nikita and Danny answered all her fears. They invited her and little John to live with them until she got on her feet. She accepted. Danny even got Sara a part time job as a waitress at the Rusty Bus. And though Sara hadn't served tables in years, she caught on quickly. To her surprise, lifting those heavy trays wasn't as bad as she feared.

She joined "The Vine," Nikita and Danny's church. She loved church, but best of all, she loved to worship. Pastor Ron was an old rocker who had a Punk garage band in his youth, but after he got saved and had, what they called, a "power encounter" with Jesus, he gave his music to the Lord and pursued a life in ministry.

Phil kept in touch with everyone at Pelican Bay. He drove up every few weeks to visit, and did so consistently for the following three years. When little John was four, Phil drove down for his birthday.

Sara was in the kitchen, feeding baby John when the doorbell rang. She opened it—to her surprise Phil was standing there, with a big ear-to-ear smile, and a three-foot plastic yellow truck in his hands. Sara grinned, shook her head, and gave him a big embrace. "Phil, that's so sweet, but he's only four, don't you think it's a little big?"

"No, No, this is perfect... I can help him. It's the first step in learning how to ride a bike—it rolls real good, see..." He bent down and began to push the car back and forth on the porch, "...and it has a place for his drink and snacks... and take a look at this...." Phil squeezed a little horn on the steering wheel.

"Johnny missed you Phil, he will love it!" Sara was overjoyed. To their surprise, they were falling in love.

Nikita held both of them in prayer often. I guess it worked, because at Johnny's birthday party, when Danny was cutting the cake, Phil announced, "Well, I have good news—I resigned my position."

"What do you mean, what are you going to do?" Sara said.

"I love this little town so much: the water, the beach, and the people. I've decided to move here."

"You're moving here?" Sara's heart pounded. Her hands started to sweat.

Nikita stood there, smiling, looking back and forth at Sara and Phil.

"I made the move—I joined the Sheriff's Department, right here in town. That's where I was last week: driving down for interviews and looking for a place to live."

"Why didn't you say something?" Sara asked.

"I didn't want to get my hopes up—until I knew for sure. I start Monday. I also bought a house... at the end of the street, near the beach."

Danny jumped in, "You bought the Miller's place? Isn't that a duplex?"

"Yes, I thought I could earn extra income, renting out the other half."

"When did you do that?" asked Sara.

"Oh, this is the exciting part; I call it my mustard seed faith. Remember about six weeks ago when we were walking on the beach?"

"Yes, I remember," said Sara.

"Well, it was for sale, so I inquired, on my way out of town. I made an offer on the spot and they accepted. Escrow closed yesterday."

"And the job, when did you get it?"

"That's the cool part—I believe God wanted me to move here, so I stepped out in faith and bought the house. The problem: No job—that's scary. But get this, the day I signed the escrow papers, I ran into the Sheriff, at the diner next to the real estate office. He told me they're adding a detective position to the force and said I should apply. The next thing I knew: I had the job. There you go—my seed faith miracle. What do you think of having me for a neighbor?"

Sara sat there, stunned.

Nikita jumped in, "That is the best news I've heard all week. God is so good! Let's pray and thank the Lord for his faithfulness."

They reached across the table and took each other's hands. Sara took hold of Phil's hand and squeezed it gently, letting him know how she felt about the move. Phil returned the squeeze. Nikita and Danny peeked out of one eye, as little John hummed a beautiful melody while painting on his plate with SpaghettiOs.

10 NEW BEGINNINGS

Sara and Phil had a hilarious relationship. Year one: Sara went to Phil's house every chance she had. She told Nikita, "He needs my help; you can't rent a place if it's a mess, and a good tenant will help him out financially."

"Sure he does," said Nikita, "you're such a good helper. I'm sure Phil has *nothing* to do with it?"

"It's not like that Nikita. Phil is not interested in me."

"Sara you're so guarded. Sometimes I think little Johnny is your safety net."

"What are you talking about?"

"Sara, it seems like every time you and Phil get too close, you quickly turn your attention to Johnny."

"I don't think so Nikita!" She paused. "Is it that noticeable Niki?"

"You think? We love you guys and I think you'd be the perfect couple!"

"I need to take it slow." Sara nodded and walked away.

Year 2: Sara told Nikita, "I think it's time Johnny and I get our own place. You guys have been so gracious to us.... I hope it doesn't put you in a bind."

Nikita hoped she was going to announce their engagement. "No, it's ok, I think it's good for you guys. We love you."

"We love you too. You're like a sister to me, and Danny is amazing, he's like my little brother. You helped me put my life back together."

"Did you find a place?" as if she didn't know.

Bashfully, she said, "Yes, I thought I would rent Phil's duplex," grinning, "I saved a bit—I think we can make it work."

"You and Phil?"

"No silly, Johnny and I... *financially*—Besides, Phil needs a good tenant."

"Sure he does..." chuckling.

"Come on Nikita—we're friends."

"Sure you are.... *Come-on Sara*, when are you guys going to stop dilly-dallying and tie the knot?"

"What are you talking about, NIKITA? We're *good* friends."

"Emphases on *good*?"

"Oh stop it! I need to pack—I want to move this weekend."

"This weekend? Hum, well I can help."

Sara walked over and gave Nikita a big hug, "I love you guys so much."

So they moved over the weekend. Things were good for the first six months—until the day Phil popped the question.

"Sara, I can't take it anymore."

"What Phil, what can't you take?"

"This arrangement.... I mean—you know how I feel about you... don't you?" Phil sat there with enamored eyes and sweaty palms.

"*How* do you feel Phil? I know you *care* about me—Johnny and I care for you, too." Sara was fishing, wanting Phil to open up and say what was in his heart. She could see it in his eyes, but he could never say the "L" word.

"I love you Sara.... I think I did the first moment I saw you in the hospital. There, I said it—I LOVE YOU—it's done." He paused for a second, clearing his throat, "Well, I'm not quite finished—I think we should get married— this silly wall between us has to come down. So what do you think?"

Sara sat there, dumbfounded. "What wall Phil?"

"That wall." Phil pointed at the wall separating the duplex.

"Oh. *That wall....*"

"Come-on Sara, I—LOVE YOU."

Finally, the words she'd been longing for. "Come here you... come here, and kiss me."

Three weeks later, they got married, and the wall quickly came down between them, literally! The wedding was memorable, Danny was the best man, Nikita was the Bride's Maid, and Little John carried a gorgeous pair of silver-laced, gold rings, tied to the center of a little pillow.

Phil's vows were from the scriptures. He began to read:

"If I speak with the tongues of men and of Angels, but have not love, I have become a noisy
gong or a clanging cymbal. If I have the gift of
prophecy, and understand all mysteries and all
knowledge; and if I have all faith, so as to remove mountains, but do not have love, I am
nothing, and if I give all my possessions to feed

the poor, and if I surrender my body to be burned, but do not have love, it profits me nothing."

Phil paused. Staring into Sara's eyes, said, "**I Love you!**"

"Love is patient, love is kind and is not jealous; love does not brag and is not arrogant—Sara with this type of love—I love you."

He stopped and whispered a silent prayer, "*Lord, please let her know how much I love her.*" He continued:

"Love does not act unbecomingly; it does not seek its own, is not provoked, does not take into account a wrong suffered, does not rejoice in unrighteousness, but rejoices with the truth; bears all things, believes all things, hopes all things, endures all things... Sara—I believe in you and I believe in our love, I believe in nothing but God's blessings on our life and no matter what may come, I shall endure the darkest of situations with you. I will tread the deepest valleys and climb the highest mountains to protect you and Johnny no matter what obstacles may come our way. My love for you shall never fail... for this I know, our faith, our hope, and our love, will remain forever."

Sara, touched by Phil's words, stood motionless. Her mind drifted back to her first marriage with Todd. She thought of her loss. Like a silent movie, she flashed through the scenes of Todd's last hours.... God came through again, and gave her another new beginning. Sara's love for Phil blossomed into a crescendo of emotions. For someone who thought she would never love again, for a second time, she met the man of her dreams. Sara said:

> "Words cannot express my heart this day. God gave me a gift from heaven and sent you into our lives. From this day forward, from here to eternity, I vow to give you all my love. Through thick or thin, through high times or the roughest of days, I will walk this life with you, hand in hand."

She paused, trying not to cry,

> "I vow to support you as God leads us to fulfill our destinies. I vow to be a listener and to bear any burden that may weigh heavy upon your heart. I vow to support you, comfort you, and to be your soul mate—a partner in building our future together. I pray that today will be the first day of the rest of our lives, and together, under the banner of heaven, we will forge out a Godly marriage that will light the path to peace in all that we do. I love you Phil, and

give you my heart, will, and desires. I lay them down at the feet of our union."

The wedding was perfect, and the reception, spectacular. Danny prepared the most incredible feast, with ice sculptures of hearts and angels, rows of sweet pink shrimp and clusters of king crab legs. Nikita played the Wedding Song (there is love) by Peter, Paul, & Mary, on her guitar. Sara and Phil danced the night away. At the stroke of midnight, they were ushered into a limo—off to Key West where they spent a couple of nights before heading out to sail the Caribbean, on their honeymoon.

The first weekend they were away, the town of Pelican Bay had their annual "Taste of the Bay" festival. Danny demonstrated the art of Ice Carving at the foot of the pier. Danny is an exceptional ice carver. He carved ice on the side for local catering events on the island. He told Caps, "I feel like Michelangelo trying to find the beauty trapped inside a 150-pound block of ice." Every time Danny fired up his chainsaw, the local kids gathered around the back dock of the Rusty Bus. With wide-eyes, they watched Danny slash, cut, and chip away at the block, until all that was left was an angelfish or a dolphin staring back at the children.

He'd tell them, "Kids, this is what God does in your life…. He peeks deep down inside of you and wonders about your potential. Like a skillful ice carver, he removes and shapes your life, carving out a path for your future— for your destiny. Inside each of you is a beautiful sculpture longing to get out. Don't ever give up on being the best you can be. God has a wonderful plan in store for you, He want's *super dudes!*" About the time the sun started to reflect through the clarity of the ice, was the moment he turned and said, "Just like the sun light reflecting through the ice, so God's glory reflects through you." That's why Danny loved this town. It was small enough for him to make a difference in the life of those kids.

Today was Johnny's turn. He loves to hang out with Danny and the pier was the perfect place to go. The little town of Pelican Bay loved this day. Folks came from all over... as far north as the Suwannee River and Alligator Pass and as far south as Big Pine and Bonita Beach. Main Street was packed, cars everywhere. Even old Bob Miller turned his vacant lot, behind his hardware store, into a half-day parking lot. Mangrove Avenue closed down and turned into a street fare. Up and down the street, along the pier, and the little boardwalk, local town folks and businesses set up booths and kiosks to sell their tasty southern tidbits and sea-crafts. Mrs. Crawford put out her own version of Key Lime pie. She called it Citrus Cream Pie, made from sour oranges, key lime, and chiffon. Marry Perkins sold her famous peach chutney and Larry Jen-kins's booth was filled with smoked mackerel, sea trout, red snapper ceviche, pickled shrimp, and a homemade salsa, he called Fisherman's Fire. Danny setup his demonstration the night before at the base of the pier—everything except the 150-pound block of ice.

Dan and Johnny headed for the corner getting ready to cross the street. Two little kids stood next to the streetlight with their mom. They were standing by a large box with a sign taped to the side that read: "Free Puppies." Hearing, what sounded like yaps coming from the box, Johnny ran over to investigate. Peering inside, he found seven pairs of big black eyes encased in thick balls of spotted fur staring back at him. Seven little Border collie pups were wrestling and biting each other in a playful romp. Each had one eye on Johnny and the other on their siblings. They playfully pawed and chomped at each other's tails and legs—all except one. Sitting alone, tucked into the corner of the box, away from the rest of the litter, was a fluffy black and white puppy with one blue eye. He sat there gazing up at Johnny.

"Danny... he likes me," Johnny's eyes were about as big as the puppy's, "Can I pet him?"

"Go ahead little buddy, he sure is cute."

Johnny reached down and cautiously extended his little hand to the puppy's head and rubbed him between the ears. The puppy instantly responded with licks and paws. He seemed to smile as he softly nibbled on Johnny's palm.

"I think he likes you," said the mother.

Johnny kept petting and playing with the little guy. "Danny, can I have him? I'll take really good care of him... I'll feed him and everything."

"Oh, I know you will little dude, but we need to ask your mom."

"Yes sir, but she's not here, right now."

"She'll be back tomorrow, maybe this kind lady will hold onto him for a day?" Danny glanced over at her and smiled, "We can get her number and call her tomorrow." Danny was in a real pickle—separating Johnny and a puppy tugged on his heartstrings. Nevertheless, he knew this was Sara's call.

The owner of the puppies, scribbled her number on a piece of paper, bent over and handed it to Johnny, "Here you go Johnny... you take this and call me tomorrow after you talk to your mom & dad. I'll hold on to him for you.... I promise I won't give him away."

Johnny reached out and gave her a big hug, "Thank you Ma'am, thank you so much."

"Say goodbye Johnny, we need to go."

"Okay Danny. Don't forget we need to ask my mom... you *and* me," Johnny reached down, pressed his face against the puppy, and said, "Bye Blue... I'll come by to-morrow and take you home."

Dan and Johnny stood at the corner, hand in hand, making their way across Main Street towards the foot of the pier. Johnny kept looking back at the little puppy. In turn, the puppy's head popped over the edge of the box and stared back at Johnny.

"So what's with the name, where did you come up with Blue?"

"Oh that's easy... he has one blue eye. He's different from the other puppies. He's like me."

"What do you mean Johnny?" Dan was puzzled by his answer.

"He's the only one with an eye like that, right?"

"Yep."

"So, it's like my birthmark. None of the other kids have a mark like me, do they?"

"I understand," said Danny, "It's like you guys were made for each other."

"Yep, that's what it's like."

As they were walking towards the pier, Danny said, "Johnny, I'm going to take you over to Caps while I set up my demo, okay?"

"Alright... it won't take too long, will it?"

"No, only a few minutes."

Johnny stood next to Caps waiting patiently for Danny to get done setting up.

Caps is a rusty, one-legged fisherman—an angler with a rugged wrinkly face like old leather. He has fished these waters for over fifty years. He sat back in a rocker on the other side of the pier, telling kids the story of how he lost his leg—fighting off a great-white shark. He laughed, and coughed some, before pausing, then peered down at the wide-eyed children surrounding his chair, spread his arms wide open, and crashed them together, yelling, "Chomp... just like that, boys, he locked onto my leg—throwing me about like an old rag-doll.... I wrestled and fought for my dear life, until Smitty saved me with an old rusty spear. Because of Smitty, I am here to tell the tale." He reached into his pocket and said, "This tooth right here is the tooth that Doc McCracken, God rest his soul, pulled out of my hip." He held up a big black 3" shark tooth.

Mesmerized by the size of that tooth, the kids chimed in: "Can I see it.... Let me hold it.... No, I want to hold it." Just when he saw the eagerness in their eyes, he passed around that old black tooth. It was the size of a child's fist.

The kids loved Caps story. Year after year, he sat in the same spot, telling the same story—but for the town it was a tradition—he became a living legion. Not bad, for an eighty-year-old angler. Some of the parents standing there, sat on that same boardwalk years earlier, were now transported back to their own childhood reflections of that moment, and the feel of that rugged tooth in the palms of their hands. Johnny, on the other hand, was a million miles away. He wasn't thinking about sharks or ice carvings, he was thinking about that black and white puppy with one blue eye.

Yes, the day seemed like every other holiday in Pelican Bay, until a flashstorm rolled in. It came in so fast, in seconds the sky turned black as sackcloth, and the rain poured down in sheets. Everyone started running. Danny dropped his ice carving tools and ran over to Caps. "Where's Johnny, Caps? Which way did he go?" Danny stopped in a panic, looking around in all directions.

"I don't know Danny. He was just here a second ago."

Danny wiped rain away from his eyes. "Caps, you need to get out of the rain.... I have to find Johnny!"

Then he heard the sound of tires screeching behind him. Seconds later, the blaring honk from a car's horn sounded. Alarmed, he turned and saw Johnny, soaking wet, standing next to a car that had skidded in the rain. He ran over to Johnny. The rain kept pounding. Danny's heart was in his throat, he yelled, "Johnny, STAY THERE! DON'T MOVE!" As Danny approached, Johnny was staring at the front of the car, crying. When the rain started, Blue jumped out of the box and ran towards the street. Johnny saw him and ran over calling out, "Blue... stop!" Blue kept on running. That's when the car came—the driver slammed on his brakes trying to avoid little John. He missed him by inches, but hit the puppy, instead.

What he didn't see was a seven-foot angel standing between Johnny and the car. Nathan sensed something happening in the heavens, as if a tempest had arose. The storm was unusual. Something strange was taking place.

Nathan sent Raphael to protect the child, while he soared into the sky, seeking out the source of the storm.

The Lord spoke to Nathan, "Let it be. The child must learn to call out to me."

"Yes Lord." Nathan shot back to the pier, scouting the area for signs of the enemy. Nathan's team of angelic warriors never left the side of Sara or her child. They understood the call of God and the depth of this mission.

Danny stood behind little John, resting his hands on his shoulders. Johnny broke away from Danny's grip and ran to the puppy. Staring down at little Blue, he lifted up his eyes to heaven and cried out as loud as he could, "*Please Papa, Please... stop the rain!*" Instantly, the rain stopped, and the sky cleared, as quickly as it came in.

Danny was dumbfounded... "Johnny?"

Little John continued his plea to his Papa, "*Please* give me back my puppy, *please, Papa, please.*" Then Johnny reached down at blue's lifeless body and said, "**Get up puppy... Get up**; *your Papa loves you too.*" At that moment, the breath of God entered Blue. He began to shake and shiver, from the top of his head, to the end of his tail. The puppy lifted up his little head and started licking the sides of Johnny's face. Johnny reached out, grabbed a hold of Blue, and placed him on his lap. Blue licked his hand.

"**Danny, he's alive!** My Papa gave him back to me."

Overcome, Danny said, "Yes John, I see!"

Johnny glanced up to heaven, "Thank you Papa, thank you! I love you so much!"

Danny knelt down and whispered into Johnny's ear, "Who's your Papa?"

"God silly.... My mom taught me to say, 'My Father, who's in heaven...' when I pray. So, that's what I always do. Besides, He loves me, and likes it when I call Him Papa."

Dan just smiled, "I know He does. Come on let's get going." A good-size crowd, soaking wet from the rain, was standing around the car. They all saw what happened.

The owner of the pups came over and whispered in Danny's ear, "What just happened? I swear that driver hit that puppy."

"The boy likes to pray..." he said, "and God likes to answer."

"Yes, but the rain? It stopped... and the puppy... I'm sure it was dead, no.... I mean it couldn't survive a hit like that."

Danny stared into her eyes, "Jesus said, we must have the faith of a child.... That's what faith looks like."

"I guess so." She stood silent shaking her head, then said to Johnny, "Well, he's yours now, if you still want him?" She glanced back at Danny, "I got a feeling they're inseparable!"

"I think your right." Danny said, "Come on little buddy, get your puppy, let's get packing, and head home."

"You mean it... I can take Blue home?"

"Yes Johnny, I just don't know what I'm going to tell your mother."

"Oh, she's going to love him... look at that eye... he is a good dog. Besides, God made him better."

"What can I say to that? Come on let's get moving." He was staring down at Johnny as they headed back home, dripping wet. Johnny had Blue tucked under his neck in a big embrace. Blue, on the other hand, was licking Johnny's cheek continuously, his tail wagging franticly—he had found a home.

Nathan and Raphael walked slowly behind them, praising the King for His wisdom and strength. They were so amazed at the power, and simplicity of faith. Nathan turned to Raphael and said, "My friend, ever since the garden, I have stood in awe watching the Master's plans unfold through mankind—yet, as I stand here today—the miracle and simplicity of faith, enacted through the human spirit, is as fresh today, as ever. To witness it through a child... leaves me speechless. Oh, if these Kingdom people only understood the power residing inside of them, they could move mountains."

11 TRANSITION

Things moved along in Pelican Bay, the honeymoon now over, Phil and Sara settled into their home as a couple. Danny did his best explaining how Johnny prayed for the rain to stop—and it did, and how a lifeless puppy, lying in the street, was brought back to life. Sara had history with the miraculous, angelic visitations, recovery from death, and prophetic insight. She understood the depth of intersession and the power of God. Yet, hearing of God moving, so simply, with no struggle, no wrestling with one's thoughts, or theological conflict, made the beauty of this miracle amazing—a simple move of God at the request of a child.

The years went by for the Rosen family. The boy grew from a child—they called Johnny, to a young man who wanted to be called John. He was quiet, and often seemed to be a million miles from home. He loved his family deeply, and Phil was a good dad to John. Prayer and long walks on the beach were a big part of John's life. He didn't talk about it much... but it was a part of his fiber. He was drawn to the water, and became closer to his "Papa God."

The docks were the perfect place to grow up. At fifteen, John's interests changed. His best friend Bryon, a tall boy from the neighborhood, dragged him down to the boatyard every chance he got. Every day, John and Bryon raced to meet the boats coming in from the previous night's catch, running and jumping over tackle, nets, crab traps, and empty buckets; they camped out in an old wreck-of-a-boat they called—Methuselah. What would you expect? They were teens, and this was their harbor.

South of the pier was the entrance to Higgins marina. It was one of the few deep-water marinas left on the gulf coast of Florida. As you entered the marina, past the ship's store, behind the high n dry, was the place, the boys called, the bone-yard. Methuselah was tucked away in the back corner of the bone-yard. She was a 1957, 54 ft., wooden cruiser. Her hull was torn asunder during a storm back in the seventies. In her day, she was a beauty, with a massive mahogany interior, teak deck, spacious cockpit, large galley, and, of course now, a huge hole in the starboard hull of the boat.

The wear and tear on this old vessel was beyond repair, but not for the boys. They'd climb up the ladder through the hole in the hull, making their way through the cobweb-infested galley, they transformed into a fort. It was here they talked of dreams... of sailing the seas, and traveling around the world in Methuselah. This was also the place where John came to pray and talk to his Papa. Praying for John was natural. He learned at an early age how simple it was to talk with Papa God.

As a youth leader at church, John's role was to teach the children how real God can be in their everyday lives. For him, the key to understanding the simplicity of prayer was found in the realization that prayer is just talking to God. He wanted them to 'get it' while they're young and full of promise.

John took a handful of five and six year olds out to the playground behind the church. They sat in a circle on the grass. There, he'd pose a question, "Who can tell me how to pray?"

A cute little girl, with long curly red hair, and a pug nose dotted with freckles replied, "You take your hands, like this..." she paused for a second, demonstrating to all her classmates how to put their hands together, then she continued with a giggle, "...and you touch your nose, then close your eyes, and lower your head, like this," she giggled again as she peeked out with one green eye.

Another boy, eagerly raised his hand up and down, jumped in, as if he understood the secret to prayer, "I know... I know..." he said smiling.

"Go ahead Tommy," John replied.

"Our Fader," he said with a lisp, "whose art is in heaven... hey, wait a second," puzzled, he asked, "Hollow be his name...? Does God have a hole in His name?"

"No Tommy... God doesn't have a hole in His name," John's smile turned to laughter. Then all the kids started rolling on the ground laughing. Even Blue got in, on the act. All you could see were little giggling faces peering through legs, fur, and grass stained knees tucked with-in a pile of children. When Blue saw all the excitement, he grabbed his rubber bone and began weaving in and out of the kids; jumping into the air, he pawed everyone. That's when they wrestled him to the ground.

"OK kids, calm down," John said. He called for Blue and grabbed hold of his bandana collar, giving him a big bear hug, he said, "Listen kids, do you want to know the secret to praying?"

"Yea," they all replied, "I do…. I do too," they said.

"OK, I'm gonna tell you. But first, I want to ask you a question. When your tummy hurts and you're lying in bed because you don't feel good, how do you tell your mom?"

One little boy said, "I put my head under the covers and cry out, MOMMY—COME HERE… Pleze"

Another kid said, "I grab hold of my oldest blue blanket and walk down the hall and jump into my mom and dad's bed. Then I put my head on my mom's shoulder and tell her, 'my tummy hurts….' She gives me a big hug and holds me till I'm better."

"Yea," Tommy said, "and she gives me some of that icky pink stuff too—yuck!"

John continued, "…And when you want to play, or color with your dad, what do you say?"

The little girl with the curly red locks chimed in, "I go and sit on my daddy's lap and give him a BIG kiss and a hug, and I say… 'I love you daddy…' and he says, 'I love you to baby,' and I say, 'would you please color with me?' Yep—he always does—too!"

"You guys are smart. This is going to be too easy." John glanced over at his dog, "You see that old dog, Blue?"

"Yes," they replied.

"Well, did you know that Blue got hit by a car when he was a puppy and died?"

"NOOO," they replied with wide-opened eyes.

"It's true," said John, "It happened when I was about your age...."

The kids listened intently as John explained what happened on that strange rainy day when God brought Blue back to life. He asked them, "Do you know how I prayed?"

"No," they replied.

"It's easy. My mom taught me that prayer is simply talking to God. She taught me that God is my father and He cares about everything in my life. So, I always call God 'Papa,' and that's all I said, '*Please Papa, Please...* stop the rain.' Instantly, the rain stopped and the sky cleared. Then I said, 'Papa, *please* give me back my puppy, *please papa, please.*' After that, I knew in my heart, my Papa heard me, so I reached down and said to Blue, '**Get up puppy... Get up**; *your Papa loves you too.*' You know what happened next?"

"What happened?" they whispered.

"He got up, and shook all over.... The Lord brought him back to life."

Yes, prayer in the Rosen household was extremely important. John's mom was a prayer warrior, and Nikita was a true intercessor.

The times were changing and John was on the verge of getting a glimpse into his future. It was on a hot summer day in 1996 that John's outlook on life began to alter. He was in a state of transition. Behind, a child that loved to play in the boat yard, catch fish, and imagine, in front, a man eager to embark upon the world. There stood John, a teen, caught in the middle. He had so much hunger, eagerness, and desire. He was constantly thinking about tomorrow. He had no idea, that morning, when he joined his mom and Nikita for breakfast, it was going to be a day to be remembered, a milestone.

John sat at the kitchen table listening intently to his mom and Nikita talk about the craziness in the world. As usual, Sara and Nikita got together for their Morning Prayer session, and like always, they talked and prayed about the issues of the day. John sat attentively, as they went on about President Clinton and his sex scandals—as if he didn't hear enough about it in school last year. He listened as they described the thousands who lost their lives in Rwanda, and the earthquake that hit Japan. "*My God*," he thought, "*5,000 died.*" At sixteen, he had a deep heart of compassion. For the first time in his life, he was faced with the reality of where the world could be heading.

He sat stunned, when he heard about a Japanese Cult injuring thousands of innocent people with nerve gas. It was John's wake-up call. He started to see the big picture. They talked about AIDS, and the millions who died so sadly.

Nikita said to Sara, "I can't believe what happened in Oklahoma—the bombings!"

"So senseless," Sara said, "even justice is backwards. Take OJ for example... a battered woman killed, and no one held accountable."

"I know," said Nikita, "don't you think that all these things are just the beginning of sorrows, the birth pangs that Jesus spoke about? It sure seems like it to me. Are we on a path of no return?" She paused, "Take the assignation of the Israeli Prime Minister... What was his name...?"

"Yitzhak Rabin," Replied Sara.

"I mean... here's a little country—Israel. Which, by the way, is about three times the size of Miami and one-third the size of Maine; it's smaller than Lake Michigan? Did you know it was almost destroyed two thousand years ago? ...In 70 AD, the Jewish people were scattered across the globe.... Then, nineteen hundred years later, Satan tried to wipe them off the face of the map by that demonized madman Hitler. You know it was only a couple of years after the holocaust that they started to return to their own land and become a nation again."

"It was May 14th, 1948," Sara interjected.

"Yes, and in 1967, during the six day war, the Star of David, once again, flew over the city of Jerusalem; first time in 2,000 years... and now... we have this assassination... and the crazy terrorist uprisings... it goes on and on."

"Nikita, we need to pray."

John thought, *"The Last Days... End Times... I wonder if we are really that close."* He got up from the table and walked outside, feeling numb.

Then that so familiar, still small voice, filled his mind, "Go to the place I have called you... Go to a people called out by my name...." It was the Lord, but this time the voice of God was loud... and clear.

Hesitantly, he replied, "Yes Papa, but what can I do? Who am I? I'm just a kid!" There was no response... simply silence. "Papa," he said, "Jesus, can you hear me?"

John ran as fast as he could down the boardwalk, through the docks, past the high n dry, until he came to Methuselah. He stopped for a second to catch his breath. He made his way up the ladder and through the hole in the side of the boat. He crawled back to the galley, and plopped down on a bunk he had fixed up with an old sleeping bag and a couple of stuffed pillows.

He leaned against the pillows, quietly praying, until he fell asleep. That's when the Lord spoke to him. He had a dream. He dreamt he was standing in the middle of a desert. Around him was nothing but dryness; so dry the ground was like a sea of hard, cracked soil, layers of wrinkled broken skin—a leper's landscape of dirt and dust. He thought, *"Even the cactus and foliage is dying."* In his dream, he was standing there, wondering why... there was so much death.

The voice of the Lord echoed in his dream, "John, do you see this dry and desolate place?"

"Yes Papa."

"John, do you believe I can breathe life into this desert place?"

John stood there... silent for a moment, and then said, "Jesus, you can do ALL things."

"Yes, my child, but people are the conduit of my power."

"What do you mean?"

"Listen John, and understand the days that you are living in. Listen to me John. You are one of my chosen vessels! I alone am God, the First and the Last, there is no other. It is by my hand that the foundations of the earth were laid. The palm of my right hand spread out the heavens. I spoke and they came into being. Come closer and listen to me. I am going to tell you plainly, so that in the season of the Latter Rain, you will understand, and act."

The words of the Lord penetrated his being. Like thunderous waves, they vibrated throughout his mind. "Yes Papa, I hear you...."

"Yes, but do you *really* see the dryness of the land?"

The desert heat bore down on him. The Lord was indeed, his 'Papa', but he was also God Almighty... the creator of all things. John trembled at the sound of His question, and then said, "Yes, Papa, I think I do..."

"John, look again...."

Fear and awe gripped his heart. He peered at the desert before him.... Then he stopped, and knelt down, examining the soil. Startled, and visibly shaken by what he saw, he fell backwards, landing on the palms of his hands. Between the cracks in the desert floor, faces cried out to him in anguish... hundreds and thousands of faces—all, crying out for rain. He heard the sound of the wind, but the sound changed; it wasn't the wind at all. It was the mingling cries of parched dying souls trapped beneath the crust of the earth. John's heart started to pound uncontrollably. He jumped to his feet and looked up to heaven. Tears merged with the dirt on his face. He cried out desperately, "Lord, they're everywhere.... What can I do?"

"Call for rain John! Call for the rain!"

"I can't Lord, I... I don't understand."

With a father's heart the Lord replied, "John, you have to see, what I see...."

"Forgive me Papa... I'm just a boy."

"Why do you say, 'I'm just a boy'? I have given you a new identity. On this day, you will have the heart of a Rain King. No longer will you say, 'I am just a boy.' Today, you have become a 'Son of Thunder.' The time will come, when you will hear my voice and you will ask for rain. In that day, in the days of the Latter Rain, I will pour forth showers, thunder, and lightening, unlike the world has ever seen. You will bring life to a dying people. You have been given the gift to see the anguish in my heart, and understand the refreshing power of My Spirit. Now look to the west, above the mountain tops, and tell me what you see."

"It's a cloud, a single cloud, no bigger than my fist."

"So is my fist in your hand. Now ask for rain!"

John stood there, trembling under the desert heat. His mind filled with cries in the wind. In desperation, he surveyed the sea of faces, trapped in the desert floor. A surge of strength and power began to move through his body. He stared at the cloud in the distance, and then cried out, "Papa, bring it down—send your rain!"

Instantly, above the mountains, the sky became black. Thunder, roared and echoed, throughout the heavens. Lightening filled the sky; like a luminous force of glory, pushing an endless blanket of clouds above the desert. The rain came—thick, dark clouds of rain, sweeping across the desert. The landscape was in a deluge of water. The surface of the desert became a sea of mud. The land began to quake, as a multitude of mud-caked people climbed out of their miry desert prison. They all stood up, lifted their arms to heaven, and praised the God of all Glory, as the rain-washed away the mire that clung to their souls.

John dropped to his knees with his head to the ground, and grabbed handfuls of mud, tossing it in the air. His heart slowly began to still, as the peace of the Lord rested upon him. He sat there in his dream, quiet before God, crying and worshiping in the mud. The energy flowing through his body caused him to shake. The sky cleared, and the landscape turned into a plush green fertile field. The desert had been transformed into a valley of vegetation. John watched as he saw hundreds of thousands of people, lining up in columns and rows—like a battalion of warriors, ready to march. They moved across the valley in perfect unity. In their cadence, they sang a new song, *"Worthy is the Lamb of God. Worthy, worthy, worthy, is the Lamb of God."* With every step they took, the land thundered in submission. With every verse they sang, the trees clapped their hands. John sat there, breathless... praising God for His greatness, mightiness, and tender mercy.

He felt as if he was caught up to the heavens—before the throne of God. In that moment, he saw a vision. It was a vision, within his dream. He stared, as he saw the sun rising in full strength, coming up over the horizon, behind the mountains, and beyond the desert. The sky was brilliant with orange and golden light. The sun filled the sky with its power—spurting and shooting out flames of fire. Then, walking out of the midst of the sun stood Jesus. He was standing above the valley, taller than the tallest of mountains. His hands were outstretched, and his face shined as the sun in full strength. His eyes were as a flame of fire, and His voice, as the voice of rushing waters.

Jesus spoke to John, "Walk with Me and see My salvation. Walk with Me and know that I am God, for the day of My great outpouring is coming. The day of salvation is at hand. The winter rain has ended, and the summer rain is coming upon you. For behold, across the land, as far as the eye can see, I am raising up a people like unto Me, to usher in the day of the Lord - the day of the Latter Rain."

John, filled with the Spirit of God, stood there astounded. He saw himself walking at the foot of Jesus, as a child would walk in the steps of his father. Jesus lifted up his hands, and the earth began to quake, the sky behind him started to roar, and the brightness of His glory began to shine and fill the heavens around him.

The Lord spoke to John again, "Get up and prophesy to my people—tell them the rain is coming—the days of captivity are over—for the Latter Rain of My presence shall pour across the land and shall never end, until they see Me, face to face. In that day, I shall say unto them; sing for joy, O heavens! Rejoice, O earth! Burst into song, O mountains, for I the Lord, have comforted My people, and in their sorrow I will have compassion. You, John, shall say to them, 'Come out you prisoners of the desert! The Lord, this day, is giving you your freedom!' They will be my sheep, grazing in green pastures that once were bare. They will never hunger nor thirst again. The searing sun and scorching desert winds will not reach them anymore. I the Lord, in My mercy, will lead them beside the cool waters—I will make the mountains flee, and highways will be raised above the valley. For my people will return to me."

John woke up.... His heart was pounding. He felt overwhelmed by the dream. The presence of God was all over him. Dumfounded, he sat with his head bowed, and said, "Papa, this is too big for me."

"No my son. What is impossible with man—is possible with Me. Do not fear or feel anxious. Hold my words in your heart. The season of rain is yet to come. Rest in my peace, and walk with your eyes wide open."

The words of God filled his mind, as waves of peace calmed his spirit. He left Methuselah and walked along the boardwalk, when he ran into Bryon.

"Hey John, where have you been?" Bryon said.

"You wouldn't believe me if I told you."

"Come-on... where?"

"Oh nothing, I was down at the boat praying and I fell asleep."

"It must be the heat." Bryon said.

"It's hotter than you think Bryon; it's hotter than you think!"

"You're telling me, bro. Let's get a cone."

"Sure Bryon, I could use one."

So, John and Bryon headed down the boardwalk, towards the General Store in search for some ice cream, but in the back of John's mind, all he could see were images of faces trapped within the desert mud.

12 CAPS

Summer now over, the little town of Pelican Bay started to get quiet again. Local traffic drove the spring and summer months, but the heart of the season started in the winter. All the northerners or 'snowbirds,' as the islanders called them, fled their homes in the north for winter vacation time on the island. Caps loved the summer, not too many tourists and all the kids were around. In his hay-day, he made his living trapping Stone Crab. The season ran from October 15 to May 15, and Caps always sold what he harvested. These days, he supplemented his income, selling smoked mackerel, pints of smoked-fish dip, and Red Snapper ceviche, to tourists and local restaurants. Caps didn't enjoy the season as in seasons past. It was hard for him to move around. He sat up in bed and nested his head in a pile of pillows. Time was getting short.

In the back of the Ship's Store, next to the High n' Dry, was a little bunkhouse, Caps called home. Thirty years ago, he partnered with Stew, to help him run the marina Smitty had left him. Smitty was Caps best friend. Smitty didn't believe his son could run the place alone. Before he passed away he asked Caps to help Stew out. One leg or not, Caps was determined to give Stew a hand. Caps' ship and sea knowledge was endless. He forgot more, than most people know, about fishing, trapping, seamanship and boating.

Most days, Caps sat outside the ships store in his rocker, offering his services as a consultant. Day after day, he sat giving free bits of wisdom, or troubleshooting some issue for a boater. When he wasn't verbally fixing things, he was beating Stew at a very aggressive game of checkers. Time went on and Caps got weaker. His age caught up with him. Instead of Caps taking care of Stew—Stew became Caps caretaker. Caps had been bed ridden for several months. In his day, he could fix anything: small engines, diesels, mercs, and the list goes on. He could work with fiberglass, or seam a sail, and he was a legendary fisherman. Nowadays, he felt worn and tired.

Lying in bed, Caps prayed, "Dear Lord," he said with a raspy cough, "I hear you calling.... Please watch over Stew when I'm gone. He's not as young as he thinks. Be with Johnny, he is going to need your help. Thank you Lord for giving me a full life." He opened his eyes and called out for Stew, "Stewie, give me a hand, will you?"

"What's up Caps, can I get you something? Are you hungry?"

"No, no, I'm fine.... Can you get my Bible off the nightstand for me?"

"Sure Caps, whatever you need," Stew felt uneasy, "Here you go Caps, do you want me to read to you?"

"No thanks, not now. Just listen for a second...." Caps thumbed through his old King James Bible and pulled out an envelope tucked between the pages of the book of Acts, "Take this letter for me."

"Okay Caps." Stew reached across the bed and took the old worn envelope in his hands, rubbing the worn fiber between his index finger and thumb.

"I want you to give this letter to little Johnny Rosen. He's a good boy, and I'm about done here."

"Come-on Caps, you're the strongest guy on the docks. You got years left in you."

"Now listen Stew, your dad and I were best friends."

"Yes Caps, I remember."

"Stewie, it's time for me to join your Pops."

"Don't talk like that..."

"I love you Stew. Thank you for taking care of an old seadog all these years."

"What do you mean? You take care of me! Look at this place; I couldn't have done it without you."

"Listen Stewie, when I'm gone, I need you to help that boy Johnny with his sea legs. I'm leaving him that old sailboat out back. You know the one I'm talken about ...that old Cal."

"I know Caps."

"That Cal's a fixer-upper; he'll be fine, if you give him a hand."

"Sure Caps, I'll take care of him."

"I'm leaving my fishing boat and the other two out back for you; they're old, but in good shape. And my traps, they're for you too. Please Stewie, don't forget to give him that letter—It's important." Caps stopped to catch his breath, "I'm kinda tired now, I think I'm gonna take a nap."

"Sure Caps, you go ahead, I'll take care of things." Stew walked over towards the dresser and grabbed an afghan off a chair in the corner. He turned around to wrap Caps up, but he passed away. Stew reached over and took hold of his hand, "I'm gonna miss you, ya old timer." Tears streamed down his face, "It just won't be the same without you." He reached over and closed Caps eyes. He laid Caps Bible down on the nightstand and covered his face with the blanket. "Your ship has sailed my friend. May God's face, shine upon you forever. Say hello to my Pops."

Caps died, and John's life started to change. Alone in his bedroom, John read Caps' letter.

Dear Boy,

I never told you what happened to me ten years ago, the day you saved Blue in the middle of that flashstorm. I was there when it happened. I remember it as clear as day. You were a little boy, so excited about that little puppy. Out of nowhere, it swooped down in buckets. One minute the sun was out and the next second—drops of water the size of my thumb.

Johnny, you did something that day that changed my life forever. I lived a tough life. I had no patience and was hard as nails. I could get in a fight quicker than a pit-bull dog.

But something happened that day. When I saw you running towards that dog and you looked up to heaven and told the rain to stop... and it did.... Then I heard you pray. I saw your puppy... as dead as could be, but when you prayed, and he came back to life - it did something to me.

I never prayed before. I never thought the good Lord had time for me. But, when I got home, I sat at the edge of my bunk and ask the Lord to give me a heart like yours. I wanted faith like a child. You showed me that, and you know what? He answered my prayer. That very moment he touched my heart, and came into my life.

I didn't think he would forgive me, but He did. Witnessing your faith opened my heart. I want you to know how thankful I am. I have been watching you grow most of your life, and you have been such an inspiration to an old man.

Keep the faith Johnny. Stay strong, even when tough times come! God has *something in store for your life. Keep your eyes on Him and He will carry you.*

Now remember, like I told you, the tourists always go for the Grouper, but the fisherman go for the Red Snapper. Remember to always follow the cloud and not the crowd. Think about what I am saying. The Lord will give you wisdom.

Now, I'm leaving soon. I want you to have that old Cal sailboat of mine. Stew's gonna help you with your sea legs. It's a good boat, but it's gonna need some work.

Remember that shark tooth I had. In the back of the drawer on the right side, in the galley, you'll find it. It's for you.

Bless you Johnny.

Your Dear Friend Caps

Reading Caps letter touched John deeply. Every chance he had he spent at the marina learning what he could from Stewie about seamanship. He learned to repair the hull and deck. He fixed every inch of the boat, working on the hatches and portholes, the bulkheads, rigging, and sails. He was becoming a pretty good seaman. Stew took him out on the water and they sailed for hours.... Methuselah had faded away and the old Cal became Methuselah II.

During the next two years, John had that sailboat in prime condition. Even Bryon helped. They both joined a sailing club and often made overnight trips up and down the coast. Those weekend trips made Sara quite nervous. Their first trip was down to Tampa Bay where they docked at Bonita Beach Marina. It took all day, stopping at Egmont Key along the way. They made their way under the skyway bridge, and headed into the heart of Tampa Bay. Soon their adventures took them to the Keys. It was an endless summer and those weekend trips turned into weeklong adventures... but on those long trips, Phil insisted on coming along. The boys didn't mind. It was one thing to do an overnighter—another thing to do it for a week.

Those years were quiet for John. He was still involved in church and kinship groups. He still taught the kids, though not as often. He never told his mom about the dream he had two years earlier. He thought of it now and then, but God's voice seemed quieter.

13 18

July 11, 1998

John's 18th birthday was a big day at the Rosen house. Sara wanted this birthday to be the best ever. She set her coffee cup on the patio table and leaned in, "Nikita it's been 18 years...."

"I know," Nikita reached across the table and took hold of Sara's hand, "Have you ever talked to him about it?"

"No, not yet..." She paused, twisting her hair in frustration, "I don't know what to say."

"Tell him the truth... the best way you can."

"Today is the day. I think he is old enough...."

"Why today?"

"Today, he's a man...."

"Sara, John's faith is strong. The Lord will give you the right words to say."

"I guess you're right." Sara stirred her coffee back and forth, "I'm uneasy.... Do you want to go shopping? I need to get a couple more presents for John."

"Sure, sounds good. Danny won't be back for a couple hours. He loves to shop."

"Let's go. Phil said they won't get back till after six."

"Ladies day out shopping... I can't wait!"

The drive back from Orlando was long and tedious. Traffic was heavy and getting out of Orlando took forever. Phil went down for the National Sheriffs' Association's conference and decided to make it a three-day weekend and take John along. Perfect timing, they left Friday morning, went to Universal that night, spent all day Saturday walking the exhibits, Sunday at Disney, and then headed back Monday—just in time for John to be ambushed by a surprise birthday party.

"John, you want to drive? My back is killing me; too much walking I think."

Surprised, John said, "I thought the Tahoe was off limits... being an official government vehicle and all?"

"Ah, what the heck... it's your birthday." Phil pulled over to the side of the road and tossed John the keys, "Don't speed," Phil said with a grin.

"Come-on Dad, give me a break." John got in the car and fired up the ignition. "Why are all these people driving so SLOW? Why don't they get over?" John tried to merge into traffic.

"Ok son, hit the lights.... They'll let you in."

"Are you sure?"

"Yes," Phil said, smiling.

As soon as John turned on the lights, all the cars slowed down and merged into the center lane. "Too easy," John said.

"What do you mean?" Phil admired the excitement in John's eyes. He was so proud of him, a good kid. He graduated early, taught Sunday school, and was totally devoted to Christ, and his family.

"Check this out: a second ago—stuck in traffic, then, with the flip of a switch, everyone moved out of my way."

"They call that, authority." Phil reached into his jacket and pulled out his badge. "Do you understand the difference between power, and authority?"

John glanced back at Phil puzzled, "I think so."

"Well, tell me what you think."

John never thought about it before, "No, you go ahead...."

"Okay, see that corvette?"

"Yes Sir."

"When it comes to power, this Tahoe is no match for a corvette. We both have a V8, but there are 400 horses under the hood of that Vet. My Tahoe... a measly 200 horses." Phil paused a second, "Now picture this car with no lights, no police insignia, or anything, a plain-Jane SUV."

"Okay."

"Do you think the driver would pull over if you rolled down your window and asked him to stop, in a plane-Jane SUV?"

"No. He'd probably think I was nuts."

"Right!" He reached over and handed John his badge, "What about now? What if you waved this at him?"

"Ah, I think I get it."

Phil could see it in his eyes. "Now, explain it to me."

John was trying to arrange his thoughts... then he said, "The power of the car is only relevant as long as the two opposing forces are on the same plain or equal in authority."

"Very well said, go on."

"If someone comes along with greater authority, like the authority behind your badge, the person with less authority **must** yield to the greater authority." He looked at Phil for a nod or something, "That's right, isn't it?"

"Correct! So, when you turned on the lights, all the cars behind you recognized that symbol of authority, and moved out of your way. So, when Jesus said, 'All power and authority, in heaven and on earth has been given unto me, now therefore go….' what was he saying?"

"Wow, I get it. When we go out serving Him, we are not only backed up by His power, but more importantly, His authority; no matter what may come, we can fight… and conquer… through that same authority—having heavens' badge of victory standing behind us."

"Understanding the authority in Christ is one of the keys to success in your walk." Phil was excited that John was beginning to understand it.

John said, "Like this?" He flipped on the lights, turned on the siren, and sped down the highway. In seconds, he cleared a path down I-4. He glanced over and watched Phil's face turn pale… his eyes bulged out as big as marbles. All John could do was laugh.

Phil clutched the sides of his seat, "Ok buddy, that's enough… pull over…." When John eased up on the gas he said, "Funny… John."

"Sorry Pops, just playing." John slowed down, making his way to the right lane. "But, you have to admit dad, that was a blast."

14 HAPPY BIRTHDAY

18 years since the accident... 18 years since John was miraculously saved and ushered off to Nikita's house by an angel.

Danny came by early. He offered to cook dinner. Everyone loved when Danny cooked. He had a way in the kitchen that made everything seem easy. John's favorite meal—tacos! His absolute favorite taco—green chili pork! Danny went down to the Chop Shop, picked up a Boston bone-in pork butt, rubbed down with adobo, smoked paprika, macerated poblano peppers, and Himalayan pink salt, and then slow-smoked it over hickory. Nine hours later, after basting with a sour orange Mojo, he pulled it and let it simmer in a roasted hatch chili tomatillo sauce. "A few toasted corn tortillas, some avocado, jalapeno pickled red onion, Queso Oaxaca and cilantro, and I think we have it," mumbling to himself as he stirred the pork with a wooden spoon.

Sara hung balloons, ribbons, and a banner that read "Happy Birthday Big Boy!" in the living room. "Nikita, you think this is a bit childish?"

"Not at all hun, he's going to love it."

Nikita was putting the finishing touches on a double fudge cake when Danny walked in with the pork, "Hey babe, what's cooking? Any word from Phil?"

"I just spoke to him, they should be here any minute and this is supposed to be a surprise."

Phil turned onto Gulf drive when John asked, "Dad, you don't think mom is going to try to surprise me again? Remember last year? Hilarious."

"Your Mom? No, of course not! Remember to act surprised when you walk through the door," said Phil with a grin.

They both started cracking up, "I don't think I can take another million balloons…. Besides dad, I'm 18!"

"Grin and bear it, if you can."

They made their way down Mangrove and pulled into the driveway. "Dad, lights are off and the blinds are closed... Better put my face on."

Sara scrambled and ducked behind the sofa, "Shhh, he's coming!"

Danny snuck around the back and ran down the street to get the bus. They told Sara and Phil they were selling the VW so they jumped at the opportunity to buy it and give to John for his birthday.

The door slowly opened. "SURPRISE!" they all shouted.

"Oh man, I can't believe you threw me a surprise birthday party," John said as he walked up to hug his mother.

"Happy Birthday sweetie!" She gave him a long bear hug.

"Thanks mom!"

Nikita walked up, "Come here and give your Aunt Nikita a big hug!"

"Hey, where's Danny? Something sure smells good...."

Seconds after Danny finished tying a big ribbon around the bus he walked through the door, "Hey John, hope you have your hunger on! Happy Birthday buddy!"

They all sat down to eat Danny's taqueria feast. Nikita leaned into Sara and said, "Are you going to tell him?"

"Not now. After the big surprise." Sara didn't understand why it was so hard for her to talk about his birth. *"Maybe it was Todd?"* she thought. In reality, it was the weight of having such an incredible promise hang over someone's head.

"Come on John, let's step outside for a second," said Phil, "I want to show you something."

They all followed Phil as he made his way to the front door and slowly opened it. Sitting in the drive was that old Rusty Bus. It had a big ribbon tied around it with blue balloons, and "Methuselah III" engraved on its wooden bumper.

John's eyes lit up, "You got to be kidding me. I can't believe this! Are you giving this to me?"

Danny chimed in, "I was thinking about selling when your mom and dad talked me into selling to them... *for you.* Check out the bumper dude. Awesome isn't it?"

"Awesome! I always loved that bus." Teared up, John turned and gave his mom and dad a hug.

"You just drive careful," Sara said.

"Oh, he's a great driver," said Phil, looking at John with a smile.

Nikita looked around at the group and said, "Come on, let's blow out candles and eat us some cake. They headed back in the house, John with the keys to his new VW in hand.

John turned to his mom, "Mom, Dad, I made up my mind."

"About what?" Sara had a strange feeling in her stomach.

"I have been doing a lot of sailing and... well, I have been planning a trip, a sailing trip."

"Sounds good. Where do you want to go? I can take some time off..." said Phil.

John interrupted, "No Dad, not like that. Bryon and I, we want to take Methuselah II down to Belize."

"Belize? That's out of the question. Do you know how far that is, and how dangerous a trip like that can be?"

"I know. I did all the planning, and I graduated early. Bryon and I are a solid team and I know we can do this." He paused, "Come on mom. This is a once in a lifetime experience... Please!"

"Johnny, I don't think it's a good idea. What if something happens? How would we know? What would we do?"

"John, let's talk about this later. I'm sure there are much safer places you two can sail to. Besides, hurricane season is not the time to sail the Gulf Stream."

"I gave this a lot of thought, been planning all summer long, and I promised Bryon."

"John, a trip like that is serious business. Please, let's discuss this later, Okay?"

"Alright, but wait till I show you my plans... all charted out."

"I'm sure it is son, now let's eat some cake."

Nikita and Dan sat listening to the conversation. Then Nikita chimed in, "Hey, why don't we take Methuselah III down to Pancake Beach and watch the Sunset?"

"Great idea Nikita," Sara said. So they all headed down to Pancake Beach in the Rusty Bus with John at the wheel.

15 WISDOM

Sara's persistence and Phil's unrelenting wisdom had an impact on John's adventurous desire. He decided to hold off on his sailing trip till the following summer. A good thing too, the 1998 hurricane season had the highest number of storm-related casualties in over 200 years. The first tropical cyclone, Tropical Storm Alex, developed on July 27, and the season's final storm, Hurricane Nicole, became extra-tropical on December 1. The strongest storm, Mitch, was tied with Hurricane Dean for the seventh most intense Atlantic hurricane ever recorded.

Mitch was also the second deadliest Atlantic hurricane in recorded history.

In late October 1998, Hurricane Mitch struck Central America, leaving more than 11,000 people dead, destroying hundreds of thousands of homes and causing more than $5 billion in damages. Sustained winds reached 180 mph, while gusts were more than 200 mph. After making landfall in Honduras on October 29, Hurricane Mitch moved through Central America before reaching Florida as a tropical storm on November 4.

"Dad, I'm glad we listened to you and mom. We could have ended up like the Fantome. Mitch would have crushed us like a bug." The horrifying story of the Fantome was imprinted on John's mind. He imagined what it must have been like for captain Gavan March to maneuver a 71-year-old 282-foot ship into a force-10 cat-5 hurricane.

"She was a beautiful sailing vessel John.... And yes, I am glad you took our advice."

"31 people died that day. They say it literally disappeared, like a ghost ship.... I guess it cracked in half, you know, like its bow and stern were on top of two fifty-foot waves, and the empty trough in the middle... just cracked—then sank."

"Well thank God you weren't there," Phil said. "Let's finish rinsing these sails and get something to eat. I think we should double check your SatNav, VHF radio, and EPIRB (emergency radio beacon) this afternoon."

"Dad, Stewie said we should get an amateur radio. He said he would teach me how to use it. What do you think?"

"I agree, now let's get some food, I'm hungry!"

Phil and John were seated on a weatherworn picnic table in front of Skinny's Burger Bar when his cell phone rang.

"Phil Rosen. How can I help you?"

"Sheriff, this is Sue. I know this is your day off, but you're needed down at the Pier."

"What's up Sue?"

"A fisherman pulled up a trash bag with, what appears to be, a human skull inside."

"Did you say skull?"

"Yes Sheriff, a skull. Steve is on the scene."

"I'll be right there. Contact Deputy Steve and tell him not to disturb the contents." Phil hung up and said to John, "I need to go. Can you take the trolley back?"

"Sure dad, not a problem. Is everything okay?"

"It's fine; tell your mom I might be late for dinner."

Phil arrived on the scene and gazed at the contents of the bag. "Here we go again," said Phil. "It appears to be from an animal sacrifice.... But what's with the human skull?" Lined up in a row, on the side of the pier, were a human skull, a bone that appeared to be a human forearm, 3 headless chickens, and the headless cadaver of a goat. "Steve, I assume you called in the forensic team?"

"Yes Sheriff."

"Recently dumped I bet."

"Why do you say that?"

"Well to begin with, the chicken feathers are still intact, and there's very little decay on the goat.... This is a fish feast, but nothing has been eaten.... Look, there at the base of the skull, it's burnt, but you can still see singed cartilage. Probably black magic, maybe Santeria or Palo Mayombo."

"Strange Sheriff. You seem to know a lot about this stuff." Deputy Steve was visibly shaken.

"Last year I joined a task force outside of Tampa. Two metal boxes were found containing a calf's tongue and 100 rusty nails, one in front of the courthouse and the second in front of the county jail. A short time later, under a bridge next to old highway 41, we found a makeshift ritualistic sacrifice site. We found bones, skulls—both human and animal, machetes, and knives with dry blood still on them, pots filled with rocks, shells, and sticks... and a baby buck antler... also covered in blood."

Steve was spooked, "This is crazy Sheriff."

"Steve, it gets worse. That same month ARM Investigators, with the Animal Recovery Mission, contacted us. They found a second site off a dirt road near 301 near Little Manatee, very similar to the one we found only this site had horse and human remains. It turned out that the human remains were of a child. We knew it was black magic due to the amount of blood needed for their sacrifice."

"Did you catch the perps?"

"Yes, our investigation led to the arrest of a Palo Mayombo Tata, the spiritual leader, for the murder of the missing child."

"You think this could be related?" the Deputy asked.

"Could be, that group was tied to a Mexican drug cartel. Same thing happened in the 80s. There was a couple, Juan Guzman and Maria Mendez, who engaged in human sacrifices, mutilations and other rituals that involved human organs. They believed the rites would protect their drug-smuggling ring."

"This gives me the creeps. What happened?"

"Juan Guzman, a Cuban American religious cult leader, introduced Maria to witchcraft and dark magic. He gave her the nickname 'La Madrina', Spanish for 'godmother', and initiated her into his cult, which was a conglomeration of Santería, Aztec warrior ritual, and Palo Mayombe, complete with blood sacrifices. Guzman sexually assaulted and killed drug dealers and used their body parts as part of their sacrificial ceremonies in an old warehouse near Matamoros. Many of his victims' body parts were cooked in a large pot called nganga. Juan made Maria second-in-command of his cult, and directed her to supervise his followers while he was out shipping marijuana over the border into the US."

"I hope they caught them." Steve's heart was pounding in his chest as he began to feel sick to his stomach.

"Understand Steve, this happened in Mexico City. They eventually caught her, but not Guzman. In 1989, the killings grew more frequent and gained attention when an affluent American tourist from the University of Texas, I believe, was abducted. The cult was on the run when detectives discovered their shrine. They found the same things: human hair, brains, teeth and skulls at the site of the murders. Eventually, the police found their hideout in Mexico City in May, 1989. After a shootout, Guzman and one of his accomplices were shot and killed by another member of the cult, apparently at Guzman's request."

"Same as Tampa?"

"It turned out that way. The scary part... mutilation and pain are essential to Palo Mayombo. Blood and viscera feed the nganga, manipulated with sticks as the cult leader turns to the spirit world. The demons they serve are more likely to smile on a sacrifice that died in agony. One Tata had told investigators. 'They must die screaming.'"

16 SHADOWS

ast of Ybor City, off an old farm road near highway 41, four dark figures of the underworld lurked
behind the remains of a blood sacrifice on the
Ramirez farm. You could sense their presence, but to the
naked eye: invisible. These shadowy figures weren't part of
a drug cartel... they weren't even human. They were demons led by Dharana, their ringleader.

"These dirt-creatures are so easy to deceive..." wailed
Dharana. His mangled hand moved slowly across his neck,
in a cutting motion, "...and they sacrifice to ME...."

"Meee, as well," cried another demon.

"SMACK," Dharana backslapped the underling demon sending him flying into the side of a barn.

The barn shook as Tata Ramirez said to his followers, "Nkisi accepted our sacrifice... more blood...."

Dharana laughed at the ignorant Tata, "Stir them up. Drive them to murder. I want this city painted red!"

"Yes Dharana," one of the demons wheezed, "We will drive them crazy."

A streak of blazing red light shot down from the second heaven landing in their midst. "Master Lucero," cried Dharana, "W-h-a-t... brings you... ah, your magnificence to us today?" Dharana was visibly shaken. Lucero was the principality and under lord of this region.

"WHY, Dharana, please tell me... WHY, is John Parker still alive?" With two massive black wings, he picked Dharana up by the head and swung him around like a rag doll.

"Buhh... *but master*, we tried. The prayers of the saints are strong in Pelican Bay. Those intercessors... they never shut-up, always praying! A hedge of protection surrounds the boy."

"A hedge? PROTECTION? Our master is not pleased!" He shook him more, and tossed his limp body against the side of the Ramirez house.

Ramirez felt a rush of wind blow across his face. "Nkisi– Come!" His eyes filled with a rage.

One of the other demons cried out to Lucero, "Master, watch this..." he flew onto the body of Ramirez, possessing him and causing his body to fall to the ground, convulsing violently. The drums sounded out and Tata's followers started to shake and dance.

"ENOUGH!" said Lucero. He waved his black bat like wing at Dharana, causing his contorted body to slide towards him, then said, "Obvious to all Dharana, you are too weak for this assignment! I want this boy dead... **do you understand ME! DEAD!**"

"Yes master... we will finish him, *a plan is in motion,*" Dharana trembled.

"You failed us twice—a third time and you will be dismembered."

"But master, the Holy angels... Nathan and his team are powerful, and God's glory surrounds them," Dharana cowered as he tried to crawl away.

"Glory? Holy angels? Nathan? There you go again Imp, making excuses. Get it done... or you will have the same fate as John Parker! I am leaving Yemaya with you, *again,* until this assignment is complete."

Yemaya passed through the ground where they stood and slid into Dharana's face like materialized black sludge. "My turn Imp!" He pushed Dharana aside.

"But my plan... It's already in motion!"

"We will see Dharana," Yemaya's blood red eyes penetrated Dharana's blackened mind causing him to squeal in agony.

"Get it done Yemaya, or I will be back and dismember all of you!"

17 AHOY

John and Bryon loaded the last of their supplies into Methuselah II, "Bryan, let's check off our provisions.... Beans?"

"Got it."

"Peaches?"

Bryon shuffled through the galley stow searching. "Yep, 6 cans."

"Canned Tuna and Sardines."

"Got it."

"Instant Soup?"

"All set."

John continued, calling out the rest of the canned goods, dairy, breakfast items, meat, beverages, snacks, produce, and housekeeping items. He checked his charts, small equipment, deck and galley supplies, safety equipment, fishing gear, and spare parts. "Bryon, I think we're ready! Let's get a good night's sleep and head out early. The weather is amazing all week. First stop Naples!"

Morning came quickly. John didn't sleep a wink. The anticipation was overwhelming. "Mom, Bryon is meeting me at the dock in an hour, I have to go."

"I'm just worried John." Sara leaned on the kitchen counter, "Johnny, make sure you call me every night!"

"Mom, it's going to be fine." He walked over and embraced his mother, lifting her off the ground with a big bear hug, "Under control mom. I LOVE YOU!"

"Sara, he'll be fine. The boys are well prepared for this trip." Phil believed it, but his insides were in turmoil.

Nathan, Raphael, Cayla, and the rest of their angelic team followed John and company to the docks. Nathan said to his crew, "We enter a new phase in this journey, be ready. We must say alert!"

"We're ready, Nathan. The King is with us!" replied Raphael.

"Yes, Raphael. He is with us!" Nathan, knowing he had limited information, paused to assess the situation. They all felt an increase in demonic activity in the region. "We need to strengthen our boundaries. Raphael, when you get to Boatan, prepare the Padre, and secure the mission."

"Yes Sir, he's a good and Godly man."

"I am staying with John. Cayla, stay with Sara. She is going to need you. Secure Mangrove Ave. and set guardians at the entrance to the city."

"I got this Nathan. Any word from the King?"

"No details, just that we are to stay alert and follow the plan." Nathan understood the importance of John's survival. "Remember, the King is with you!"

In one-accord they all responded, "Also with you!"

Danny handed John a brown bag, "Hey Buddy, I vacuum packed some smoked Spanish mackerel for your trip, high in Omega... and protein, of course!"

"Danny, you didn't need to do that... *But I'm sure glad you did!*" John loved Danny's smoked Spanish.

After tears, hugs, and goodbyes, on March 27, 1999, John and Bryon finally pushed off from the dock and headed south on the quiet turquoise waters of the Gulf.

Their adventure had begun. By nightfall, they made it as far as Gasparilla Island.

Docking near Miller's Dockside Grill, John called his mother, "Mom, the ride is amazing. Perfect winds... the Gulf is like rippled glass. Bryon even caught a Dolphin-fish! Dinner tonight is going to be fantastic. I told you not to worry; we are taking this trip slow and easy.... Boca Grande is not that far away."

"I'm glad Johnny. I expect you to call me at every port," Sara said, "Do you want to talk to your dad?"

"I'll catch up with him later mom. I gotta go—Love you."

"Johnny?" John had hung up. Sara bowed her head and prayed, "Papa, please be with my boy. Send your angels of protection and surround him. Bring him safely home to me."

The following morning John and Bryon reviewed their charts and discussed the trip ahead, "Bryon, I think we can make it to Key West in two or three days, and then hit the Dry Tortugas.... What do you think?"

"I like," Bryon said, "I can't wait to get to Isla Mujeres. I'm brushing up on my Spanish."

Two days later, they ambled down the coast, arriving at Key West. There, John purchased courtesy flags for visiting Cuba, Mexico, Belize, Honduras, Costa Rica, and Colombia. They weren't sure they would visit all these countries, but wanted to be prepared just in case. They also went to the Naval Hospital in Key West and received yellow fever, hepatitis A, and typhoid shots. Then they made their way through the streets of Key West, making sure to load up on plenty of Key Lime pie, from Pepe's Cafe!

After two days, they hauled anchor and headed west for a brief stay in the Dry Tortugas to do some snorkeling. "Bryon, I think, after a night in the Tortugas, assuming the weather holds true, we can make it to Isla Mujeres in four days, maybe five."

"I concur Captain!" Bryon said with a ear-to-ear grin, a salute, and a snap of his heels!"

After reaching the Tortugas they dug in for the night. "Bryon, check out that sunset—a red painted sky…. You know what they say, '*Red sky in morning, Sailors take warning. Red sky at night, Sailors' delight.*' This is truly… a sailors' delight!"

"John, can you believe this? Soon we will hit our first foreign landfall."

"Amazing! And I'm glad I'm doing it with you!!"

"Love you man!"

"Ditto bro."

Nathan sat invisible on the bow of the boat listening and relishing in the boys excitement.

After departing from the Tortugas the boys made their way around Cuba. They were debating if they should stop in Havana but decided to press on.

The second night they set anchor at 23.28° N 85.03° W between Key West and the Yucatan, outside of Cuba.

John stood at the stern when the Holy Spirit whispered to him, "*Look at the stars.... See how they shine for you....*" He watched the night sky in amazement.... Stars shimmered on the black canvas sky like diamonds on black velvet. "I love sailing at night.... I know what David must have felt when he penned Psalm 19." John recited that verse.

"The heavens proclaim the glory of God.
The skies display his craftsmanship.
Day after day they continue to speak; night after night
they make him known.
They speak without a sound or word; their voice is never
heard.
Yet their message has gone throughout the earth, and their
words to all the world."

"Incredible John, clear sky ahead, and we're right on schedule."

18 HAVANA

Across the bay from Havana, in his Guanbacoa compound, General Rafael del Rosa was meeting with the heads of Mexico's Los Vetas Drug Cartel.

The General's dark eyes locked onto Carlos, "Welcome to my humble abode Senior Carlos. We have a surprise for you this evening."

"Gracias General, for setting up this meeting. I hope you have solved our problem here in Cuba and found those scumbag-traitors that ripped off my cocaine?"

"Ah yes, and more... these scum-bags, as you call them, are in fact the main event.... All in your honor, ahh Senior

Carlos," He said with a twisted grin, "Can I interest you with a cigar and a little Rum? It's Havana's finest."

"Gracias General, tomorrow, we get down to business."

"Of course my friend, everything will be set in motion."

Underneath an old cottonwood tree in the back of the compound, a "mayombero nganga priest" was preparing for the "juegos de palo" (or palo games.) It is here that the mayombero must demonstrate proof of his power as a superior sorcerer. Tata Teodore arranged the nganga placing sticks, dirt, feathers, stones, shells, and bones into the temple cauldron. Next to him, box-drums pounded as his followers rhythmically chanted to the rumba songs of the dead.

Tata drew near. He smelled the stench—blood and decomposing organs. Inside a big cast iron pot were pieces of human bodies and a goat's head with horns. He bent down blowing rum and cigar smoke into the cauldron. Beside the caldron, were four men, on their knees, bound and gagged, with their heads hanging over a large clay trough—two on one side and two on the other.

Moments earlier, Dharana and his gang of demons descended on the compound joining the other demons already active in the ritual. Dharana cried out to the demon hoard, "Lucero has commanded! Soon, all of you shall join me.... We shall once and for all destroy the boy."

Yemaya wheezed, spewing black puss between his fanged lips. He reached out and grabbed two of the demons by the throat, "Do you understand Imps?" shaking them in the air as he spoke.

"Lucero is our master," said one of the demons.

"Yes Dharana, we are with you," said another. The drums kept pounding....

Dharana's red eyes flamed, "When these dirt-creatures sever their heads and their blood hits the cauldron, cry out to all your fellow demons in the region and bring them to me!"

The demons jumped and jerked, squealing out in slithering shrills of enjoyment; "We will... for Lucero... follow you!"

Back inside the General's house, Carlos and his new companions were finishing their cigars and rum when the General said, "I think we are ready for tonight's festivities. Let's proceed outside."

"After you General." Carlos's heart was starting to pound in his chest. They all took seats in the portico overlooking the temple.

The General stood up. Looking intently at the Tata and the Mayombero nganga priest, he raised his hand to his throat making a slicing motion. The box-drums pounded louder. Tata and the mayombero walked over to the nganga and picked up their machetes. They sang and blew smoke and rum on the blades, walked over to the trough where the four men lay waiting and started to chant. With one quick swish, they swung their machetes, removing the heads of their victims. They lifted their heads in the air, causing the crowd to go mad.

As the rumba played, they carried the heads to the sacrificial alter, and offered them up to Nkisi, Lucero, and Iku—their angel of death. Tata lifted his voice and said, "Reward us now—in triumph we behead," and he poured their blood into the cauldron.

A thousand demons from around the region descended on the compound. The General began to convulse violently. Carlos fell to the ground and slithered like a snake. Tata and his followers jerked and shook as they danced to the movements of their demonic oppressors.

Dharana lifted his voice, "Raise your wings and follow me...." In one accord, they ascended to the sky and shot out heading west towards the sea.

19 ROGUE

Cayla appeared in their room. They were sleeping. His presence shined forth a soft blue light. He bent down over them and whispered, "Awake Sara, John needs your prayers... wake up. Then his presence faded—hidden from their sight. They both woke and stared at each other.

Shaken, Sara said, "Phil, what was that?"

"We need to pray...."

"John's in trouble!"

"I know, take my hand," they both latched on the each other. Looking up to heaven, they prayed with such urgency that tears and cries filled the air. They could feel the Holy Spirit's presence, and continued to pray, longer, and harder, throughout the night.

Cayla entered Nikita and Daniel's room, overshadowing them with his light blue wings. He reached down and placed his hands on their heads.

In their sleep, they could feel the warmth of his presence. Then, in a vision within a dream, they saw the sea raging and heard the words, "Protect and Cover." In an instant, they both woke, "Danny we need to pray for John, I believe he is in trouble. We need to pray for protection and cover him with the presence of the Lord."

Together they prayed throughout the night.

The demonic hoard, under the leadership of Dharana, descended on the waters. One third took their position 165 feet below the ocean surface; one third split into two groups and flew one mile east and one mile west of Methuselah II; the last third ascended above the clouds, circling over John's sailboat.

Below Methuselah II, the lava remains of an ancient ring of fire rested on the ocean floor—a circle of hardened lava cones and domes, once active, but now lay dormant. As the demons dived deeper to the ocean floor, they latched onto the lava peaks, slashing the tops of the lava rocks, releasing hydrothermal vents from the volcanic layer below. By morning, as the 705° hydrothermal fluid poured out from the vents, the water temperature for a one mile radius rose to over 80°.

The rocking sea beneath them jolted John awake. He climbed out of bed and maneuvered his way to the bow of the boat. He stood watching the sunrise, when he noticed dead fish floating on the surface of the water, "That's strange." He hollered, "Hey Bryon, wake up. You won't believe this."

Startled, Bryon shook his head and crawled out of bed, "What's up bro?"

"Look Bryon, dead fish everywhere."

"That's weird... reminds me of a red tide.... But, the water is too blue for a red tide."

"I wonder what caused it." John pushed fish around with a long gaff.

"I have no idea," Bryon said.

One hundred feet below Methuselah II, 300 demons began swirling, faster and faster, in a swimming motion, trying to create a maelstrom in the ocean. Their action caused the surface of the water to start stirring and spinning like a drain.

Above the cumulus clouds over Methuselah, hundreds of demons began to fly in a spiral motion through the clouds. They moved like they were ascending the inside of a giant shell, forming tornado like conditions in the clouds. As they swirled up through the clouds, then out—left and right—and down again, the motion, combined with the heat of the water's surface, created cyclone type conditions. The power of what they created caused an incredible rotating updraft.

Without warning, a massive storm appeared overhead with winds climbing from 20 knots to 60 knots in minutes. *"Something is terribly wrong here,"* thought Nathan, *"I knew there would be an attack, but how?"* As the rain and wind pounded the little craft, Nathan shot up into the heart of the storm to investigate.

The sky overhead turned charcoal-black. Methuselah was engulfed in chaos. The rain beating on the deck went horizontal—a force as heavy as a fire hose. John cried out, as waves battered the sides of their boat, "BRYON, get inside and secure the cabin.... Tie everything down and turn up the radio. I am going to drop sail...." The boat rocked from side to side. The rain and wind beat John to a pulp.

"John, get back here! We need to ride this out. It's safer in here!"

"Bryon, the sail is jammed.... I can't loosen it! We're taking on water. The aft end of the boat is starting to flood."

John made his way back—they braced themselves. Cupboards in the galley were open. Can goods and supplies flew around like missiles. A can struck Bryon on the brow. Blood poured out of him, "I need a towel, I can't see."

"Hold on Bryon, let me wrap this around your head."

When Nathan entered the clouds, he saw much more than he expected—hundreds of demons swirling in the air. He reached for his sword and slashed at everything that came his way, "Father, there are too many... I'm not even making a dent!"

The storm grew stronger. The wind shrieked through the rigging. As the winds fury increased, the sea became mountainous compared to the size of this little vessel. The tops of waves blew off and mingle with the rain, filling the air with blankets of water—no visibility.

The winds rose to 70 knots. A sinister wave reared up and struck Methuselah II on the beam, sending her into a 360-degree roll. When she righted herself, the hull was intact, but her mast was bent, her rigging had torn away, and the life raft was ripped from its storage bay and fell into the sea. The mast, still connected by a spider web of wires, beat against the hull, as the boat careened in the raging sea.

With the storm now in full force, the underwater demons shot out and joined the other hoards stationed a mile away from Methuselah. Dharana cried out to the demons, "Enlarge the swells!"

Two teams of demons, 600 in all, began to increase two swells in the water, one from the east and one from the west. Both swells rose up and passed through one another; their crests reinforced each other creating a large 60-foot towering rogue-wave. It was heading directly towards Methuselah II. "If the storm does not drown him this wave will crush him like a bug," smirked Dharana.

The boys were broken and beaten down. Bryon had a busted arm. The bent mast, and what was left of the sail, was dragging the vessel underwater. "Bryon, I need to cut away the sails completely, or we're going to drown."

As John exited the cabin, the bow plunged into another large wave and then 'BAM,' the boat was hit by the rogue wave. The boom swung around and hit John in the back of the head, sending him overboard into the violent sea, and the boat into another roll.

Dharana cried out to his legion of demons, "The boy is gone! He is dead! I have defeated God. I will be exalted!!!" Overly gleeful, in his sadistic and demented mind, said, "Come, let's leave this place before reinforcements arrive. Lucero must know my greatness... I conquered Nathan once and for all!"

Nathan saw the storm-demons shoot into the sky and leave. In a panic, he looked down and saw the battered craft spinning in the water. The Father spoke to him, *"It's time to get John."* Instantly, he shot down with the speed of light.

The storm dissipated as quickly as it came in. Nathan righted Methuselah, and then dove into the raging sea looking for John.

Bryon bounced off the galley floor landing on the bunk, twisted, beaten, and unconscious.

John's limp and bruised body floated deeper and deeper into the sea. He was gone. Suddenly, from beneath the blue silhouette of his floating body, two hands reached out taking hold of him. Nathan locked on to John and shot threw the water and into the air like a ballistic missile. He embraced him with his wings, and headed toward the Island of Boatan.

20 RESCUE

Bryon sat in a foggy daze. When he came to, the storm was gone. He cried out for John, but nothing. Then he remembered John stepping out into the storm, and the rogue wave—nothing else. He broke down and cried. In a panic, he tried to piece together the events of the previous day—It was a blur, a nightmare. Lucky for Bryon, when the boat righted, he ended up on the bunk, twisted and unconscious, but on the bunk. Anyplace else, he'd drown.

The bump on Bryon's head throbbed continually. Crusted blood covered the side of his face and neck. He forgot about his broken arm until he tried to move it.

With water up to his knees, he managed to assess the damage. The cabin was a shambles. The bilge pump didn't work. Debris, supplies, and equipment where floating everywhere. All electronics and communication equipment were damaged. Not surprised, the engine wouldn't start. Bryon finally stepped out of the cabin. He spotted the busted mast and beam. Then he thought of John, pushing his way out of the cabin and into the storm—he fell apart and wept.

The boat: barely afloat. The haul: damaged. The vessel was slowing sinking into the sea. He thought, "*If I dry out the radio... then maybe....*" Then he remembered, "*The emergency radio beacon.... Why didn't I think of it sooner?*"

NOAA polar-orbiting and geostationary satellites detected the distress signal from the emergency beacon and relayed the information to the SARSAT Mission Control Center, based at NOAA's Satellite Operations Facility in Suitland, Maryland. From there, the information was relayed to the Rescue Coordination Center, operated by the U.S. Coast Guard, for water rescue.

NAS Key West Search and Rescue (SAR) unit launched its SH-3 Sea King helicopter in response to the distress signal. Three hours after Bryon set off the beacon Sea King arrived.

As the Sea King hovered over the boat a rescue diver dove into the water, adjacent to the craft.

Aviation Warfare Systems Operator 2nd Class (AW), Chris Amador, secured Bryon and communicated back to Sea King, "Alright, single survivor at 2:00, you can begin to hoist."

"Roger that. Contact Amador."

"Sailboat is moving away from him nicely." Amador swam towards the Sea King with Bryon in tow.

Lt. John Blackman responded, "Contact Amador. On its way down, holding."

"Roger that."

Lt. Blackman released the hoist. "It's going down. It's half way down. Quarter, holding."

"Roger, copy that. Moving on in."

"Roger.... Forward. Right. 20.... Hold.... Right 15."

"Got the '*ready to pick up*' signal."

"Ready. Hold.... Left, easy.... Right."

"Number two, power looks good."

"Hold.... Ease back... Ease back... Hold.... and easy right. Easy right and hold.... and easy back and left."

Amador reached out and grabbed hold of the basket and began to secure Bryon in it. The sound of the helicopter was deafening. The winds from the blades were causing the basket to swing. Bryon's heart was in his throat.

"Easy back an left... easy back an left... and... easy back an right. Hold.... Hold.... Person in... hold... taking a look.... Survivor in, clear water." Bryon was in the basket. LT continued, "Back an left.... Survivor is directly under the aircraft.... Going to verify that. Basket is directly below the cabin.... Survivor is just below the cabin door. Prepare to back it up. Basket is in the cabin door."

"Roger that."

"Basket inside cabin. Hoist release."

"Roger that. Survivor doing well?

"Out of the basket. Where's the swimmer?"

"Roger, I got my eyes on the swimmer.... Looking good."

Lt. Blackman removed Bryon from the basket, "Hey survivor, have a seat sir."

"Yes sir, OK, thank you," Bryon was visibly shaken, "But my friend, John.... He... he went overboard."

"Say again sir?"

"Yesterday, he went overboard. Did you see him in the water? We have to look for him!"

"Commander, survivor says there is a man overboard."

"Roger that. Obtain details. Calling it in."

"Yesterday, 1500 hours, vessel struck by massive swell. Vessel went into a roll. John Parker, age 18, lost overboard. Survivor struck in the head, passed out in the cabin. Survivor has one broken arm, head injury, possible concussion."

"Roger that. In communication with headquarters and Lower Keys Medical Center."

"Roger, applying treatment.

"Roger, in route to LKMC."

21 LOST

Sara sat on the bathroom floor weeping, "*Something's wrong, I know it,*" she thought, "*Why doesn't he call? Papa, please.... John, call me, please... let me know you're okay.*" Phil and Sara prayed all night long. Her mother's intuition was driving her mad. Wiping tears away with the palm of her hand, she braced herself on the tub to stand, "*I need to get my act together. What is wrong with me? Calm down Sara!*" Her imagination ran wild. Then there was the faint sound of a phone ringing... desperately, Sara opened the door and scrambled to find her cell.

Cayla invisibly stood by waiting for direction, "*Only the Holy Spirit could give her the comfort she will need,*" he thought.

"Johnny... JOHN! Is that you?"

"Mrs. Rosen? No, it's me... Bryon."

"Are you boys OK? Where's Johnny?"

Bryon, barely able to talk, said, "I tried to call earlier.... I'm sorry; I'm so sorry Mrs. Rosen. John... John is missing."

Sara was silent on the other end. Shock was setting in.

Bryon tried to get the words out, "He fell overboard. It was the storm, and wind, rain and chaos everywhere."

"Did you say '*missing*'?" She couldn't believe what she was hearing, "What do you mean? What happened to my son?"

"Search and Rescue is looking for him, right now!"

"Bryon, where are you?"

"Lower Keys Medical Center in Key West." Bryon wiped snot from his nose. "I tried Mrs. Rosen," now hysterical, "I tried to find him... but the storm...."

"Bryon, calm down. We're on our way. I need to call Phil."

"Yes Ma'am."

Sara hung up the phone. "God, God, GOD! What is going on? Where is my boy?" Frantically, she called Phil and told him about the phone call.

"Sara, hang on, I'll be right there."

Phil contacted Captain J. R. Barnet at Naval Air Station Command in Key West. "Captain, my name is Philip Rosen, Sherriff at Pelican Bay. I'm calling regarding Search and Rescue efforts for John Parker. He's lost, overboard. *He's my son.*"

Captain Barnet explained the situation to Phil. "At this time, we have not located your son. We canvassed a fifty-mile grid. There are two SAR helicopters and one SAR cutter, combing the area. Please, give me your contact information. I will contact you as soon as I have something. And Sherriff, please be prepared, it's been 24 hours since the boy went overboard."

Phil, Sara, Nikita, and Danny headed to LKMC to meet with Bryon, and join the SAR team at NAS Key West.

22 BOATAN

5 0 km off the coast of Honduras, on the island of Boatan, lies the historic Jesuit Mission of Boatan. In the spring of 1687, a Jesuit missionary named Father Francisco Bravo lived and worked with the tribal peoples of Boatan. During his stay in Boatan, he founded the mission under the crown of Spain and the Catholic Church. The worn adobe mission withstood the test of time, enduring pirates, wars, political upheavals, starvation, diseases, storms, and hurricanes.

Padre Juan Ramos, a stout fellow with a thin mustache and a small scar under his left cheek is the present day priest of Mision Santa Rosalia. Faithfully, he serves the people of Boatan, has for the last thirty years. During his ministry, he built a school for orphans, a medical clinic for the community and a small missionary outreach to Honduras and the neighboring regions.

Padre Ramos lit four candles: one for the Father, one for the Son, one for the Holy Spirit, and one for the people of Boatan. Then, he lit a small brass bowl of incense, bowed his head in prayer, and took personal communion. He did this every day before studying the scriptures, in preparation for Sunday's mass.

> "O Lord Jesus Christ, Who said to Your Apostles: 'Peace I leave with you, My peace I give to you,' regard not my sins but the faith of Your Church, and deign to give her peace and unity according to Your Will: Who live and reign, God, world without end. Amen.

> O Lord Jesus Christ, Son of the living God, Who, by the will of the Father, with the cooperation of the Holy Spirit, have by Your death given life to the world, deliver me by this Your Most Sacred Body and Blood from all my sins and from every evil. Make me always cling to Your commandments, and never permit me to be separated from You. Who with the same God the Father and the Holy Spirit, live and reign, God, world without end. Amen.

Let not the partaking of Your Body, O Lord
Jesus Christ, which I, though unworthy, pre-
sume to receive, turn to my judgment and con-
demnation; but through Your goodness, may it
become a safeguard and an effective remedy,
both of soul and body. Who live and reign with
God the Father, in the unity of the Holy Spirit,
God, and world without end. Amen.

As the Padre prayed these final words:

Lord, I am not worthy that You should come
under my roof; but only say the word, and my
soul will be healed.

A bright amber light filled his study and the presence of
the Holy Spirit fell upon him. In an instant, he was on his
knees trembling.

"Fear not Padre. From the moment you set your heart
to pray, I was sent to you."

"Who are you?" said the Padre.

"My name is Raphael. I am an angel of the Most High
God. I came to bless you, and give to you a mission of the
utmost importance." The light of Raphael's glory subsid-
ed. He reached down and cupped the Padre's face with his
hands, "Your heart blesses the Father greatly! Our Lord
and King, needs your service."

"Yes Lord."

"Please, don't call me Lord. I am a servant of King Jesus—the same as you."

Tears streamed down his face. "What must I do?"

"Come morning, as the sun begins to rise, you will walk to the beach at the foot of the mission. There you will find a young man sleeping in the sand. Our King has placed this boy into your hands. You will watch over him and care for him. He shall sleep for many days. Do not fear, nor give up hope, for at the appointed time he will wake. When he does, teach him the ways of humility, servant hood, and peace." Raphael touched the Padre on the shoulder leaving a mark the size of a coconut, "This mark is a sign of the covenant between you and your King, so you will believe these words are true." Then Raphael disappeared out of his sight.

Nathan laid John in the sand. His soothing touch revived and healed him, from the destruction of the deep.

John's eyes slowly opened. "Where a-*m* I?"

Nathan placed his hand on his head. "Peace to you John. Do not fear. The Father is hiding you in the palm of His hand. Now sleep John, sleep."

John fell into a deep sleep.

Nathan asked Raphael, "Is the Padre ready?"

"Yes Nathan. He is a good and faithful servant of our King."

"Perfect! Stay with John and give the Padre strength until the appointed time. I must go and comfort Sara. Her heart is heavy."

"The King is with you, Nathan,"

"Also with you my friend."

23 SEARCH

Sara and Phil headed into Bryon's room. Nikita and Danny waited in the visitor's area. Bryon lay there, bandages around his head, but all Sara thought about was John. She reached over and gave Bryon a warm embrace, "Are you ok?"

"Yes Ma'am. Broken arm... Bruised head... They're monitoring for a concussion. I think I'm okay. I want to help find John!" Bryon was distraught, "Mrs. Rosin, *I tried.* The storm was so bad and it came out of nowhere."

Sara placed her hand on his shoulder. "I appreciate you Bryon. We will find him." She wasn't sure. Fear set in.

Phil spoke up, "Bryon, you need your rest. We're headed to the Navel Air Station to check in on the search."

Sara's heart was breaking. She tried to hold back the tears, "*I must be strong! Lord, please help me,*" she thought. "Bryon, we'll be back when we know more."

Padre Ramos tossed and turned, then arose at 4:00 AM, "Father, I give you my heart this day. Please be with me and give me wisdom and strength." After he prayed he searched fervently for a flashlight. "There it is..." mumbling. He put on his pants and went out of the rectory towards the beach.

The blackish-blue ocean glimmered with streaks of white light under a full moon. "*It's going to be daylight soon,*" He thought. Padre Ramos scanned the beachfront looking for the boy. In the distance, next to a cluster of rocks jutting from the water, he saw what looked like a body, lying in the sand. He ran over, kneeled beside the body and carefully examined him, to see if he was alive. He ran back to the compound, grabbed an old hay wagon, and pushed it to the beach. He placed John in the wagon, brought him back to the rectory, and went to wake Sister Abby. He pounded on Abby's door.

Startled, Sister Abby woke. "Padre?"

"Yes Sister, please open the door! I need your help!"

Abby quickly put on her white habit. She wrapped her long blond hair in a white sari trimmed in blue, put on her sandals, grabbed her prayer book and rushed out of her room to find the Padre.

Padre was standing beside the wagon. "Over here Sister. I need your help."

She rushed over and peered into the wagon, "Oh Padre, what happened? Who is he? Where did you find him?" She reached down and took his pulse; "He's alive, but unconscious, maybe in a coma. We need to move him to the clinic." Abby, a young expat from the twin cities was a nurse by trade before taking her final vows and joining the order. At 24 she found her life calling. She now operates the mission medical clinic for the poor.

Padre told the Sister all about his angel visitation and showed her the mark on his shoulder. "The boy is in our hands Abby. The Lord gave us this task... to protect, and nurture him."

"Incredible Padre! Praise His Holy name. Praise Jesus." Abby's mind was swirling. "But if he is in a coma?"

"I understand Sister. This could be a long road."

"Mrs. Rosen, I'm sorry to inform you... we haven't located your son." Captain Barnet understood Sara's pain. Moments like this are hard on all involved, "I know this is difficult," he paused reaching for her hand, "We've exhausted every resource."

Sara crumbled, "Phil, he's gone. My boy is GONE!" Phil tried to comfort her. They both sat in the Captain's office, weeping and rocking, holding tight to one another.

"I'm going to give you a moment alone," said Captain Barnet. He left the room, closing the door behind him.

Nikita heard them crying and squeezed Danny's hand.

The drive back was quiet—sadness filled the air. Sara sat numb, staring out the window. They pulled into the driveway; Sara got out and walked towards the pier.

"Sara, where are you going?" said Phil.

"Going for a walk... I need to be alone, PLEASE!" It was late, the street was quiet. Sara walked to the foot of the pier, "Papa, please tell me what happened. WHY did you take my son from me?" Slowly she made her way towards the end of the pier, stopping periodically to read the memorial planks that made up the boardwalk. The café was closed. Only a couple of fishermen were on the pier. She sat crying, "Lord, please help me understand. Why? WHY?"

Nathan walked up behind her and placed his hand on her shoulder. He wasn't visible. He felt her pain and wanted to console her—tell her John was okay, that he was alive. He knew only the Holy Spirit could touch a wound this deep, and bring lasting hope.

In the midst of her tears, the Spirit of the Living God came upon her. Sara felt as if she was lifted to heaven. She looked up in amazement, wiping tears from her eyes as the Holy Spirit filled her with His presence. "Sara... it's Me, your Lord and King," Jesus spoke softly into her mind.

"Yes Lord... Why Jesus? *Why?*" She crumbled under His presence.

"Sara, do you trust me?"

"Yes, Lord, with all my heart."

"Sara, your son is alive. He's resting in the palm of My hand."

"Lord, I believe in the resurrection. I know he is in your presence. But why did you take him from me now? *He's so young,*" She pleaded for answers.

Jesus spoke plainly, "Sara. No... John is not dead. He is *alive.*" He paused and released more of his love and presence.

"*He's alive?*"

"Yes My child, he is alive."

"Oh, thank you Lord, thank you! Where is he? Let him come home to me Lord. He needs *me* Lord," She was confused.

Jesus spoke, "Sara you will see your son again, but not for many years.... He is hidden in the palm of my hand.

His time has not yet come. I am preserving him for an appointed season. The enemy will soon understand why John has been hidden. He will wonder where John came from. John's destiny will soon be revealed," He paused, "Sara, be diligent and pray like a sniper. Pray with pointed purpose and precision. Hold your family together. Strengthen the town of Pelican Bay. Take comfort Sara; understand John is in the safety of My wings. At the appointed time he will return."

Overcome by His presence, peace filled her heart. She replied, "Yes Lord, your will be done with my Johnny."

24 COMATOSE

Sister Abby wanted to rouse John, testing his neurological reaction to touch. She gently pressed on his limbs, chest, and back. With no reaction, Abby tried discomfort, as stimuli. She pinched him, "Wake-up... please wake-up. Can you hear me?" to no avail, not a sound, not even an eye flutter, just the simple movement of his chest, from breathing. She checked his breathing, "It's rhythmically sound," she said. She examined his eyes looking at the position and size of his pupils, and their reaction to bright light, and movement. His retinas were in place and his eyes respond to the light—dilating when she moved the light away, constricting when the light is brighter. She rotated his head and flushed both ears with cold water to determine if the nerves connected to the brain stem functioned. "Padre, the boy is definitely comatose. I'm going to check his reflexes to determine if there is brain or spinal cord damage."

"Thank God you're here Sister!" Padre Ramos continued praying.

Cayla stood behind Abby, watching her as she continued to examine John.

"Padre his reflexes are good—responsive. I am going to need a series of lab tests. I need to check his red and white blood cell counts, liver function, and look for possible heart and lung disorders." Abby's call to action was quick and decisive. She monitored his heart rate, blood pressure, temperature, and oxygen levels in the blood. "Padre, I'm going to stay with the boy. The next 6 hours are critical."

"Sister, we can take turns." Padre Ramos felt helpless, but believed the boy would be fine. He had the mark to prove it! "Sister, the best thing I can do is pray."

Abby elevated the boy's bed slightly, put on a breathing tube, an IV, and then sat down next to him to pray.

On Tuesday, April 20, 1999, John became comatose. He was 18 years old and stayed in a coma for 20 years. Every day, Sister Abby tended to John's needs, rotating him every 3 hours to prevent bed sores, feeding him through a tube, pumping his stomach to remove excess acid, gently exercising his joints to decrease the chance for blood clots, giving him eye drops because he couldn't blink, empting his urine bag, changing his catheter, and bathing him.

Padre Ramos slept on a cot in John's room every night for 20 years. He watched John as he slept. "What is your name? ...Where did you come from? ...Why are you here?" endless questions flooded his mind, "How old are you?" One thing he did understand: God delegated this mission.

The Padre and Sister Abby took their tasks seriously. Their devotion to this assignment became their life's call.

Sara waited for John's return. Every day she walked out to the pier, to the place she received the promise, and prayed for his safety. She believed in her heart the promise was true. Phil wasn't so sure. He believed in Sara, but struggled with doubt. "*I think the love of a mother is stronger than logic,*" he thought. When he did bring up the subject of laying him to rest, she would have nothing to do with it, "I know what the Lord said to me Phil! I believe... and know in my heart John is alive. Somewhere, he is waiting, to come home to me."

Nikita prayed with Sara for John. They were extremely close—inseparable. Danny wasn't sure. At times, he sided with Phil, other times he sided with Sara. They all wanted to believe. But as the years went by, it became harder for everyone to believe, except for Sara.

25 CHANGE

I sland isolation can be a good thing. In the years that followed, the world became a very different place. On September 11, 2001, two years after John's coma, Al-Qaeda, under the leadership of Osama bin Laden hijacked four planes targeting the World Trade Center, the Pentagon, and the White House. Two planes struck the Twin Towers; one plane took out Wedge 1 of the Pentagon, and the forth was found in an open field 80 miles outside of Pittsburgh. Altogether, over 3,000 people and 400+ police officers and firefighters lost their lives. Anthrax-laced letters followed—sent to various media and government officials. Several died after handling the letters.

In response to the attacks, the U.S. formed the "National Commission on Terrorist Attacks." U.S. and British forces launched bombing campaigns against the Taliban government and al-Qaeda terrorist camps in Afghanistan. Bombings continue on a daily basis.

On January 23, 2002, the "National Movement Restoration of Pakistani Sovereignty," a terrorist group, kidnapped Daniel Pearl in Karachi, while conducting research for a Wall Street Journal story. Nine days later, they decapitated Pearl.

Three months later the Space Shuttle Columbia exploded, killing all on board. By spring, the war on Iraq began. On April 9, 2003, the U.S. coalition seized control of Baghdad. By December 13 they captured Saddam Hussein in a small bunker in Tikirt.

On December 26, 2004, a tsunami occurred in Southeast Asia, following a 9.3 Richter scale earthquake, in the Indian Ocean. Two hundred and ninety thousand people died, creating one of the greatest humanitarian tragedies in history. In 2005, Hurricane Katrina struck the Gulf Coast of America, inundating the city of New Orleans with water. Over 1,300 people perished in one of the worst natural disasters to strike the United States.

By 2006, the global populace rose dramatically. The U.S. population hit three hundred million, a gain of one hundred million people in forty-two years.

On June 2, 2007, authorities thwarted a terrorist plot to blow up JFK International Airport in New York City. Four terrorists were arrested and charged.

In 2009, Barack Obama became the first African-American president in history. The Democratic Senator from Illinois came into the office on a message of Change. More than one million visitors descended on the National Mall for the inauguration, reminiscent of the Civil Rights March of Martin Luther King forty-six years earlier.

On June 11, 2009, the World Health Organization deemed the H1N1 virus (Swine Flu), a global pandemic. Six years later Ebola became the fear of the day.

The economic recession deepened as jobless claims climbed above 10.0%. This occurred despite the many efforts made by the Obama administration to ramp up massive government spending, pushed by a $780 billion economic stimulus package.

On May 2, 2011, to everyone's adulation, U.S. Navy Seals killed Osama Bin Laden, the mastermind of the 9/11 attacks. The ten-year pursuit ended. President Obama declared the war in Iraq over and ordered the last combat troops to leave the country.

The war may have been over but the terror raged on. On the 11th anniversary of 9/11, terrorists attacked the U.S. Consulate in the Libyan city of Benghazi, killing four Americans, including Ambassador John C. Stevens, demonstrating the fight against Islamic terror continued.

On April 8, 2013, the Islamic State in Iraq (ISI) declared its immersion of the al Qaeda-backed militant group in Syria, "Jabhat al-Nusra," also known as the "al-Nusra Front." Al-Baghdadi said his group would now be known as the "Islamic State in Iraq and the Levant" (ISIS).

On April 15, 2013, two bombs exploded near the finish line of the Boston Marathon, killing three and injuring hundreds in a terrorist attack coordinated by two brothers associated with radical Islam. They apprehended the suspects four days following the attack.

In May of 2014, ISIS kidnaped 140 Kurdish schoolboys in Syria, forcing them into radical Islamic theology. In June, they seized Mosul's airport, TV stations, the governor's office, and freed over 1,000 prisoners. They took control of Mosul, Tikrit, Al-Qaim, and three other Iraqi towns. ISIS announced the creation of a *caliphate* (Islamic state) erasing all state borders, making al-Baghdadi the self-declared authority over the world's estimated 1.5 billion Muslims. The group also announced a name change to the Islamic State (IS). 1.2 million Iraqis were forced from their homes. By July, ISIS claimed to have killed 270 people after storming and seizing the Shaer gas field. ISIS also blew up Jonah, the Biblical prophet's tomb, a holy site in Mosul.

Then the beheadings started. First, two Western journalists, and an aid worker were brutally killed, videotaped, and broadcast throughout the world. ISIS vowed it would stop at nothing to create a *caliphate* governed by strict Sharia law. In November of 2014, ISIS released a video of the decapitation of former American Army Ranger Peter Kassig and the mass decapitation of 18 Syrian soldiers. Their brutality continued. The West became their next target.

By 2017, after the beheading of an Australian dignitary, ISIS teams made their way across the U.S. border. The first slaughter took place at a large ranch located in Texas. ISIS attacked three other ranches before being gunned down by a hand-full of laborers hiding out in the stables. The nation was outraged. Anger and indignation against the federal government ensued—for not protecting its citizens and closing the border.

One would think, after 911, the global war on terror, and ISIS, that eyes would've opened—but they didn't. One would think, after tsunamis, hurricanes, and devastating earthquakes during the first two decades of the 21st century, people would've called out to God—but they didn't. It seemed to be, the beginning of the end. A blanket of darkness covered the land. It wasn't a solar eclipse. Nor, the result of some cosmic event, though they have been commonplace the last few years. It was more elusive, obvious to some, but for many, not. Like sewage penetrating the surface of a dried out sponge, darkness breached the soul of humanity. In a single invasion, grayness was abolished. The polarity of light and darkness brought clarity to many, but rage to the rest.

Society prided itself in its openness, permissiveness, and evolutionary intellect. Now, humanity manifested its true colors. The warm fuzzy philosophy of tolerance, mingled with no absolutes, turned into an outpouring of venomous fury. Right became wrong—wrong became right. Anybody not adhering to this core belief system was not fit for society—the Global Age of Enlightenment.

The leap—too easy, once the blurriness of "everything is ok," "there are no absolutes," and "who are we to judge?" penetrated every corner of society—all it took was a push. Push it came, straight out of the gates of hell. The doorways and corridors of the deep were opened. The dominion of darkness, the demonic realm, took full advantage. The separation began. The race to destruction marched full-speed ahead. The prideful prance of the underworld marched forward, manifesting its presence on the landscape of earth. Not an earthly war—though mankind had been in global conflicts for decades—this was a war in the Heavens. Michael, the great Prince and Archangel, who stands before the throne of Almighty God defending all who call on the name of the Most High, had made his strategic attack on the prince of darkness.

Satan, the fallen foe, who once stood before the councils of the King, was cast down from Heaven and thrust to the planet earth. The portals to the Third Heaven shut. No longer could he enter, no longer was he allowed to walk the halls of the angelic, and stand before the courts of the Great King. Here, on earth, Satan made his final stand. Here, the consummation of all things came to fruition. Here, on this planet, the hearts of many were made ready for his arrival. Satan's presence on earth, now fully activated, he had no need for hiding... no need for subtleness. He was out to destroy, rule, and reign. The clock was ticking... his hour was at hand.... He knew time was getting shorter. With every tick of the eternal clock, his rage became stronger, and in his rage, Satan struck out with indignation at all mankind, and the people of God.

The nuclear holocaust, at the end of 2019, caused the world to bond under a banner of global unity. The horror of twin explosions crippled the civilized world. A dirty bomb smuggled into Los Angeles, from across the border, south of San Bernardino, devastated the U.S., and left the city of bright lights, paralyzed.

It took the nation by surprise. Islamic terrorist, under the banner of ISIS, operating out of Central America, penetrated the border, camping in the backyard of people who supported their cause. With twisted tongues, they spoke out against Israel, and engaged in every oral crusade imaginable. What did they get for their blind efforts? ...A dirty bomb planted in the heart of the city of angels.

The rage was in full force.... How long did it take to turn off their PC ideology? All the feel-good, fuzzy-wuzzy, no absolutes talk, was over. "Stop them... Kill them... no matter the cost..." was the mantra of the day. The call went out for the destruction of *all faiths*. After the Islamic extremists, Christians moved to the top of the list, at least those deemed "extreme."

"Extreme" meant believing in the literal interpretation of scripture. In the sixties, they took prayer out of school. By the mid-seventies, the ten commandants were taken off the walls of the Nations classrooms, and later the courtrooms. A strategic dismantling of Christianity in American society was underway. As the years went by, religious liberties were under assault. Christians got fired for displaying bible verses in the workspaces. Judges ordered parents not to teach their children anything the courts considered judgmental or intolerant, by the state's definition. High school students were trained to roam the halls in search of oral offences, and report it to law enforcement. Pastors faced prison sentences for reading from the Bible, or from the portions the court deemed hateful and intolerant of others beliefs and lifestyles. Ordinances were put in place demanding the review of sermons before they were spoken to congregations.

The gradual undermining of moral values in society had chipped away at the foundations of the land, and the ability to discern what was happening in the nation. The courts ruled the Pledge of Allegiance was unlawful to say in public schools, because it contained the words: "One Nation under God." Freedom of speech and religion had been replaced with freedom "from" speech and religion. All the laws that needed, to stop religious freedom, were in place.

Open persecution started, and the world united under a One World banner—a Global Community of Enlightenment. The UN had been reduced to an organization much like FEMA in the U.S. Newly elected President of the "Counsel of Ten," Damien Drakon, reorganized the institution in his cleanup campaign. He changed the name to GDRO—the "Global Disaster Relief Organization." Their new directive: to aid the world in disaster relief. The world was ready. Between the upheaval on the planet's surface and the unusual ramping of seismic activity, combined with the Global increases in destruction, caused by mega earthquakes, hurricanes, tsunamis, changing weather patterns... and terrorism, the stage had been set for a new and different international body.

After the dirty bombs hit the U.S. and Israel, mankind was hungry for a world leader to take over. They cried out for it. Damien Drakon was ready to heed their cry. By 2019, Damien stepped up to that call—his hour had come.

It happened during the World press conference covering the Drakon peace talks with Israel and the Palestine National Authority. The leaders of Hezbollah and ISIS were present and standing by ready to support this new era of peace. Out of nowhere, a shot rang out—the room was in complete hysteria. When the smoke cleared, Damien was lying on the ground in a pool of his own blood, struck in the head and arm by twin sniper bullets. He was rushed to Bikur Cholim Hospital in Jerusalem. He was pronounced dead, on arrival.

"Why would anyone shoot such a great man of peace?" was the question on everyone's lips. The world was shocked, and in mourning. He accomplished in a few days what nations, could not accomplish in decades. Anger brewed around the globe.

Robi Miller, the Council of Ten's "Prophet of Hope," and voice of the new age movement, stood on the steps of the hospital, proclaiming vengeance on the assassins of Damien. Intelligence sources implied alleged Christian radicals engineered the assassination. They linked apparent Internet sites suggesting Damien Drakon was the Antichrist. Robi Miller hated Christians. To him they were un-evolved creatures that needed to be exterminated. His favorite line was: "Bring back the Lions, these relics must go." He needed to show the world he was a man of peace—it was time to move into oneness, and chant.

With cameras on, the entire world tuned in to see the horror and loss of Damian. This became the perfect setting to move his plan into motion. As he wrapped up his chanting, calling for all the spirits of humanity to blend into one unified force, the front doors of the hospital burst open. A hysterical intern ran out screaming, "He's alive... He's alive... I, I don't understand? I can't believe it... the room... it filled with this...light. I don't know how it happened. He rose from his bed—his head was healed. His eyes... he's no longer blind. Damien is alive!" The crowd went crazy with shock and awe.

Robi Miller kneeled motionless, then, as if on cue, stood to his feet proclaiming Damien the Savior of the world. With fire in his eyes, he pointed to the heavens and blasphemed the God of the Christians. He cried out, "Avenge the evil that would have taken away our shepherd." As soon as he spoke, the sky crackled with thunder, and Damien walked through the doors behind Robi. He stood in front of the crowd and cameras, declaring, "Follow me my people, and I will lead you to your destiny. Follow me, and we shall take back this planet, and all that is ours. Follow me, and you shall see the dawning of a new age— the Age of Enlightenment has come! Now follow, and worship me... the God of the Christians is dead!" He left his audience mesmerized. Prophet Robi, the crowds, and all who watched by TV, were under his spell, bowing to the man, the shepherd and his miracle.

Damien was in all his glory. An apparent resurrection, witnessed by the entire planet, live on international TV and streamed throughout the globe, thus confirming his rightful place at the head of the table. The Council of Ten became the new governing empire. Even China backed down. Though they were not members of the Council, they retreated to the position of neutrality. Damien was the leader of the new age.

Pockets of resistance started. Christian "fundamentalists," as they were called, tried to make a stand. They refused allegiance to the Council. They didn't accept the new monetary system, refused to take an oath of allegiance, or be bio-tagged by the government! Their fight was fruitless. Many Christians had been taken into custody. Some were labeled as enemies of the Council—bounties were placed on their heads. The world had dealt with Islamic terrorism, and was not going to stand-by letting believing Christians turn back the clock on society. This was a new age, and Damien was their god.

Damien organized the world's most powerful army. He instituted the "GI" movement, a recruitment effort galvanizing the world's youth into an organization called "Guardians International." Their allegiance was to the Council, and through deception, blinded by fury, they became the eyes and ears of Damien. Together with his new

Grand Prophet of Enlightenment, Robi Miller, they went out conquering, and to conquer. Children turned in parents, sisters turned in brothers, and neighbors turned in neighbors.

The persecution that followed was unlike anything the world had ever seen... worse than Hitler... worse than Nero! Open public executions took place in the courtyards of every city. The World Council of Religions was the first to give in and agree to the Council's "Oneness Doctrine." They called it: "The New Genesis." Other *secular* denominations followed, and the people of faith scattered underground, hiding out in mountains, and obscure regions around the world. They cried out to God, ushering up prayers of deliverance to the Lord.

In spite of persecution, miracles took place amongst the believers. From a movement standpoint, they became powerless against this Global Community. Who could you trust? Without supernatural discernment, you couldn't trust anyone. Before the collapse, many in the church fell away, and followed their newfound savior, Damien, some through fear, others through disillusionment. The pre-tribulation rapture did not happen, as anticipated, and the claim-it doctrines of the prosperity movement dried out after governmental investigations. Scandal and corruption ripped through the church in early days. The web of corruption stretched to the highest places within the church. They blemished the heart of Christianity, and in doing so;

they set the stage for the new Oneness doctrine of the Council of Ten.

The decriminalization of *all drugs* was enacted, releasing a society numb to their surroundings. Sexual promiscuity increased as never seen before. Pestilence, disease, and the outbreak of unknown illnesses became rampant. In the midst of all of the chaos, the world lived under the veil of false peace. Like a frog in a pot of simmering water, they never felt it starting to boil, not until it was too late.

Demonization was everywhere. Rape, murder, and torture, became commonplace. If you weren't part of the New Society, if you were young, it didn't matter; if you were old, who cared? Whatever happens to you—is of your own making, it was your fault—you deserved it. You should have supported the Global effort. You should have joined the rest of the world. You're barbarians of the past, relics that have not evolved. Your kind is going to send the nations back to the dark ages of judgmental religious beliefs. You toss around absolutes as if God was a jealous entity, causing divisions with right and wrong, when the world needs unity. You don't understand that, we are all gods, part of one another... a single energy! Whatever happens to one happens to all. All is good; there is no wrong, because we are god.

Instead of bringing the presence and power of God to the earth, the secular church brought empty words and shallow intellect. Instead of praying, "thy will be done on earth as it is in heaven," they demonized those who moved in the power of God, and sought out His glorious presence. The cessation doctrine, a belief that the power, presence, gifts of the Holy Spirit, and offices of Christ, ceased with the apostles, had turned the secular church into helpless humanists.

The hearts of men were being tested and the silent cries from the people of God seemed a little too late. It was a season of separation.

This was the world John had missed; this was the world Sara, Phil, Nikita, Danny and Bryon lived in. The island faithful went underground. Sara and Phil turned the upper room of their home into a hiding place. Danny closed down the Rusty Bus and converted it to a free food pantry and medical clinic. Phil resigned from the Sheriff office. He told them it was for medical reasons, but in truth, he was not going to take the oath and be bio-tagged.

Every day they prayed, and at night they searched the nearby towns for people in need, ministering and finding shelter for them in the underground network, which was called "The Remnant." After the nuclear holocaust the U.S. reinstituted the borderline, just below Homestead

Florida, cutting off the lower Florida Keys from the rest of the country. Martial Law was in place. Roadblocks and inspection points were on every major highway and corridor along the border, and water access ports.

26 AWAKE

July 27th, 2019

J ohn's body was comatose, but his mind was fully engaged. He started dreaming again. The presence of the Lord rested upon him. Energy flowed through his mind causing him to tremble; he was caught up to the heavens before the throne of God.

Raphael invisibly stood next to John, with his hands outstretched over his head.

John dreamt of fields of frozen wheat covered in ice. He stood transfixed by the deadness of winter upon this endless field. He stood with his hands in the air, looking up to heaven.

The Holy Spirit spoke to him, "I Am He who walks amongst the stones of fire and casts a shadow on the face of the deep. Lift up your eyes, and behold the end time harvest. Lift up your eyes, and observe the field before you, frozen and dying, waiting for the fire of My Spirit to melt away the coldness of this world. I called you to be a prophet to My people, to bring the latter rain of My presence to the land. I am the King of kings, there is no other! You are My rain king, you are a son of thunder. What I have for you, is yours, created just for you. Now, prophesy to the wheat, and the fire of my presence will burn life into this field. Prophesy, and tell the wheat to grow before the presence of God."

John cried out, "Yes Papa, Yes. Arise and live by the power of God! By the blood of Jesus I say, ARISE!" At that moment, the sun rose in full strength and came up over the horizon, behind the field. The sky became brilliant with orange and yellow light. The sun filled the sky with its power, spurting and shooting out flames of fire. Jesus walked out of the sun and stood before the field, taller than the tallest of mountains. His hands outstretched and his face shined like the sun in full strength. His eyes like a flame of fire and His voice was like the sound of rushing water.

Jesus spoke to John, "Walk with me and behold the salvation of the Lord. Walk with me and understand that I Am God. The day of My great outpouring is here. The day of salvation is at hand. The winter frost is ending, and the summer rain has come. Behold, across the land, as far as the eye can see, I am raising up a people like Me, to usher in the day of the Lord—the day of My coming!"

John stood astounded. He walked at the foot of Jesus, as a child walks in the steps of his father. Jesus lifted up his hands, and the earth began to quake, the sky behind him roared and the brightness of His glory shined, filling the heavens around him. The fields changed, a transformation occurred. The wheat dissolved, and shoots of new wheat started to grow. Tall and strong, they shot up out of the ground, beaming higher, and higher, reaching for heaven, like a sea of grass swaying in the wind.

Jesus reached down, placed his hands on John's head, and blew on him the breath of heaven. The winds surrounded him like the force of a tornado, like the power of a hurricane. Faster, and faster it spun, until John was lifted up into the clouds, into to the eye of a storm, his hands stretched out. The storm became a cone of rain in the palm of his hands, the sky cracked with thunder and lightning... then it faded and so did the dream.

Raphael bent over John's head and whispered into his spirit, "Wake up John, it's time."

Sister Abby sat next to John watching him sleep. His body began to convulse and shake, pulling the IV out of his arm. His eyes began to shutter. He was in a violent REM state. She jumped up to check his vitals and reattach his IV. As she reached over, John opened his eyes. Abby jumped back in disbelief and cried, "My God...." She reached over and placed her palms on his cheeks, "You're awake!"

The aged Padre was on his knees praying in his rectory office when the door burst open, "Padre, he's awake! Come with me."

Padre Ramos reached for his cane and followed Sister Abby to the clinic. When they arrived, John was lying there motionless with his eyes wide open. "You're awake... I can't believe it, you're really awake," said the Padre.

John stared at them. The dream left him. It was tucked away in his spirit, his mind did not remember. He was confused and disoriented. He tried to speak, "Ma... mi..." It was hard to form words.

Abby took his hand, "it's okay. My name is Abby, Sister Abby. This is Padre Ramos. Do you understand me?"

A tear dropped from John's eye, "Ma... mi..."

"What did he say, Sister?"

"I'm not sure Padre; it sounded like he was calling for his mother."

The Padre leaned over and said, "You have been in a coma for a very long time."

"My name.... Wh-wh-ere—where... a-m I?" confused, his mind was in a fog.

"You're in the mission clinic. You're safe here." Sister Abby poured him a glass of water, "Drink this... slowly," she held the cup to his lips.

John took a sip. His mind started to clear, but his memory was impaired, and his body weak.

Abby was overcome with emotions. She cared for him for the last twenty years. 23 years old when she first set eyes on John, now in her forties, she could not believe it. She burst into tears.

John squeezed her hand, "I... it... its oh..k..." he felt these two people cared. He could see it in their eyes.

"Padre Ramos took his hand and said, "What is your name son?"

John stared back at him, silent for a moment as if he was trying to piece it together, then said, "I dow ... don't know. I can't re...mem...ber."

27 ARRESTED

Pelican Bay changed dramatically since the war. A once hidden vacation spot for tourists was now an economically depressed beachfront ghost town. In times like this, the word "vacation" wasn't in anyone's vocabulary. Persecution placed a spirit of fear in the hearts of many. The good thing about a ghost town: it's the perfect place to hide, if you're seeking safety in the midst of darkness.

Nikita burst through Sara's front door calling for her, "Sara, where are you? I need your help."

"Up here dear, I'm upstairs." Sara, now older, started her mornings much later than in her prime.

Visibly shook, she said, "They arrested Danny."

Sara reached out to Nikita, "Calm down Dear. Tell me what happened."

"They took him. He went out to help Bryon smuggle some of our brothers and sisters out of Tampa, and they caught both of them. They're holding them at the old Manatee "Re-education Center." Nikita's heart pounded; "You think Phil still has connections in the department."

"Oh dear... I'm not sure. I'll track him down."

Danny hung from a bar in interrogation room 503 with his hands and feet bound by the strength of a black nylon cord. Hanging there, he cleared his throat and said, "Cellmates listen... you must hold fast and keep the faith. God is with you!" Next to Danny swung Bryon, unconscious. His face battered and eyes swollen from beatings. Beside him was a frightened boy, no more than 15 years of age, by the name of James McEnroe—author of this chronicle.

A hefty man, dressed in a brown Guardian uniform, approached Danny, and stopped. His eyes black and hallow. The demons inside him started speaking to one another... "This one has no fear," cried the first demon. "The Spirit of God is strong in him," said the second as he began to shiver. "I will break him in two!" proclaimed the third demon.

The Guardian slowly walked over to Danny and glared at him, straight in the eye, "So, you think your God can protect you here? Don't you know, we rule the world?" a demon spoke through the Guardian.

Danny replied, "Whether He protects me now... or takes me home, I place my soul in the palms of His hands. Your time is short. The King of Glory will come and bind you for all eternity," Danny spoke directly to the demon.

The Guardian struck him in the face with the back of his hand. The demon of fear said to the demon of rage, "If you continue... surely the Warriors of Light will ascend on this place and we shall lose our stronghold."

Rage responded, "Very well, but we are coming back!" Then the Guardian turned and left the room.

28 REHAB

Sister Abby determined what the issue was with John's amnesia, "Padre, aside from his memory impairment, none of his other cognitive processes seem to be affected."

"Good thing Sister. Do you think his memory will return soon?" The Padre was puzzled. He knew this man had an important call on his life.

"I'm not sure, this is new to me. It seems to be a Dissociative Disorder... could be DFD: An individual with "dissociative fugue disorder" is unaware or confused about their identity, and will attempt to discover or create a new identity. In 1926, Agatha Christie suffered from this disorder for 11 days.

"Is that true?" said the Padre.

"Yes Father, it is!"

"Go on...."

"The Merck Manual defines DFD as 'one or more episodes of amnesia in which patients cannot recall some or all of their past and either lose their identity or form a new identity.' The episodes, called fugues, are usually a result from trauma or stress."

"I suppose being found lying in the sand unconscious and being in a coma for 20 years qualifies?"

"Yes, I believe so. My guess, something extremely dramatic happened to him, before you found him on the beach."

"Indeed," said the Padre.

"The good news: after recovery from fugue, previous memories often return intact."

John was sitting up in bed when the Padre walked in. "Good morning son, how are you doing today?"

"Very good Padre. Glad to be awake," he said smiling.

"How's your memory? Is anything coming back?" The Padre wanted to tell him about his angelic visitation, and how he found him on the beach, but decided to hold off. "Son, we should come up with a name for you? It might make it easier to communicate... until your memory returns. I hate to call you John Doe?"

"Sure, I think you're right father. You can call me Ray...."

"Well then, Ray it is."

John responded extremely well to the physical therapy. His muscle tone and reflex was strong. He was out of the wheelchair. His walking turned to jogging and by late August, he was running on the beach every morning.

29 ZULU

As the afternoon passed and the computer models absorbed incoming data from the Gulfstream flight, Jose said to the screen, "Ooooh. It's ugly," typing with two fingers in his second language:

BULLETIN 5 PM EDT SAT OCT 24 2020
ZULU BECOMING A POTENTIALLY DAN-
GEROUS HURRICANE

Centered at 15.3° N, 78.2° W, Zulu's winds were 91 knots at sea level, a Category 2 hurricane. It is moving north, 355 degrees, at 5 knots. But conditions are ripe for serious

strengthening and a turn to the
northwest and west.

In the next 36 hours expect Zulu to
become a Category 4 storm with winds
of 120 knots.

Jose said to his team, "The latest GFDL moves Zulu toward the west and southwest, and keeps it winding near the northeastern tip of Honduras. Only CLIPER continues to show a northward track. I would rather follow state of the art dynamical and global models, and forecast the westward turn." Jose moved his cursor through the models, placing the storm halfway between Honduras' Swan Island and the Cayman Islands in seventy-two hours. The Island of Boatan sat right in the middle.

Throughout the northwest Caribbean, the forecast of a Category 4 hurricane turning to the west got people's attention. Sister Abby received a call from a friend in the States, "*This hurricane is serious. Be careful and buy plenty of plywood.*" She left the clinic to go find the Padre.

By midafternoon Sunday, the Island was a madhouse. A ham radio "hurricane net" warned of a 50-foot storm surge on Boatan. Shrimp and lobster boats were running into Jamesville's deep like chickens chased by a fox. Sailboats took shelter in the mangroves there.

At 10 P.M. Sunday night, the National Hurricane Center recommended a hurricane warning for Honduras from

Limón east along the Mosquito Coast to the Nicaraguan border. Limón is 20 miles east of Trujillo on the mainland, within sight of the island of Boatan. A hurricane warning means winds of at least 64 knots will arrive within twenty-four hours.

The warning broadcast, on the late evening news, in Honduras, set off a panic. People fled from their homes in a mad rush to get to the markets for supplies. By 10:30, ice and water were gone.

BULLETIN 7 AM EST MON OCT 26 2020 EXTREMELY DANGEROUS HURRICANE ZU-LU BECOMES STRONGEST HURRICANE OF THE SEASON

During the night, Hurricane Zulu moved west 60 miles and became a borderline Category 5 storm. A Hurricane Hunter crew, flying through the clear eye of Zulu had found the pressure down to 920 millibars, the lowest reading of the 2020 hurricane season. Zulu's surface winds were estimated at 135 knots.

The mayor of Boatan, Jerry Binder, went on local radio and warned, "*This massive hurricane is an animal and it's coming to Boatan. I don't want to see anybody on the road. Please seek shelter.*"

Padre Ramos was spooked by a sudden silence. He stared at John and said, "Where are the birds? I'm used to hearing birds singing... and animal noises.... Ray, listen...."

"I don't hear anything."

"That's my point... it just became very quiet."

One of the Nuns spoke up, "I'm looking at the eye on the computer. God, the eye is heading in our direction."

Sister Abby was in the clinic. She had already begun securing the medical supplies and moving patients to a windowless room for better shelter.

John said, "Padre we have to hurry and finish nailing up the plywood."

At 7 P.M. Monday, the National Hurricane Center reported Zulu's eye was moving over Swan Island. Belize hoisted a hurricane watch, putting the entire northwestern Caribbean, from Mexico to Honduras, on alert. The storm was moving west-northwest at 8 knots with steady winds of 157 knots, and gusts of an astonishing 200 knots. The center now warned of rainfall over Honduras of 15 to 20 inches.

On Swan Island, 40 miles NW of Boatan, a small military contingent from Honduras took refuge in ditches. Cows were blown into the sea. Three concrete buildings tore apart as if blasted by an atomic bomb.

John stood next to Abby in the shelter. He looked at the children and saw the fear on their faces. He glanced back at Sister Abby, turned, and walked out of the shelter.

"Padre, Ray is leaving... It's not safe out there."

The bands were hitting the island with 60-knot winds and the slanted rain felt like bee stings. John approached the beach beside the mission. The Padre stood in the distance holding on to a Palm tree.

John gazed up at the black turbulent sky and cried out, "Father God, help us, now!"

Raphael stood behind John as he cried out to heaven.

The long forgotten voice of his Papa flooded his mind, "John, I hear your cry and have felt your tears in the night. I Am He who walks amongst the stones of fire and casts a shadow upon the face of the deep! Look up John and know My salvation is at hand... even at the sound of your voice."

John's mind filled with memories. He saw himself as a boy praying for his Papa, to silence the storm. He saw himself standing next to his dead puppy, speaking life into his new fury friend.... The scene changed and he was praying as a young man in Methuselah, at the old boat yard.... He saw the dream he had, and the cracked desert floor.... Again he heard the voices of those crying out between the cracks. He remembered the words of Jesus, "Why do you say, 'I'm just a boy'? For I have given you a new name, and on this day, you shall be called My Rain King, and on this day, no longer shall you say 'I am just a boy,' for today, you have become a 'Son of Thunder.' The time will come, when you will hear My voice, and you shall ask for rain. In that day, in the days of the Latter Rain, I will pour forth, for you, showers, thunder, and lightening, unlike the world has ever seen. You shall bring life to a dying people, for you have been given the gift to see the anguish within My heart and the refreshing power within My Spirit. Now look to the west, above the mountain tops, and tell me what you see...." Then the Lord spoke to John, "Today is the day! Today the power of this storm will be in the palms of your hands. Speak to the storm John, and tell it to cease. SPEAK JOHN!"

The Padre watched, as John raised his arms up to heaven. The power of the wind almost lifted him off the ground.

With his arms raised, John cried out in a powerful display of the Holy Spirit's presence, "I command you Zulu... I command you in the name of the King, BE SILENT.... Waters BE STILL!"

Instantly, as if a massive hand covered the 160-mile wide hurricane and smothered it, "poof," it was gone. A blanket of peace fell over the region.

The island became silent. Padre Ramos fell to his knees. Moments later the sound of birds were heard in the background as John turned and walked towards the Padre. "Padre, give me your hand. It's okay now. The storm is over."

"Thank you my son. What did I just witness?" The Padre was shaken.

John looked into the Padre's eyes. He placed his hands on the Padre's face and said, "My name is John." Then he looked up to heaven and began to pray for the Padre. "Papa, I thank you for sending me to this mighty man of God. I thank you and praise your name for bringing me to this Holy sanctuary. And I ask you now to stretch out your heart of love and fill Padre Ramos with your glory."

A mist from heaven drifted down and covered them. The Padre was overcome with peace and the love of the Lord. As the dew washed down the Padre's face and arm, he felt the heat of Almighty God. He tore off his shirt and watched as the mark on his shoulder dissolved before his eyes.

Raphael manifested his presence through a brilliant blue and white light. He stood before John and the Padre. "Padre Ramos, the Heavenly Father is greatly pleased by you and Sister Abby. Your name is chronicled in the books of heaven. Your service to the King is a memorial to all generations. Receive the blessings of your God." He reached over and blessed the Padre. The Holy Spirit fell and burned upon the Padre's heart. He trembled to the ground as electricity surged through him.

"Thank you Lord," cried the Padre.

Raphael turned to John, "It's time for your return."

Tears were streaming down John's eyes, "I must see Sister Abby before I go."

Raphael responded to John, "In two days' time, at the dock on the east side of the island you will find a Bahamas-flagged yacht. Its name is 'Sleeping Beauty.' Go there; the owner will be expecting you. It's bound for the port of Manatee." Then Raphael disappeared.

Jose was dumbfounded. The specialists at the National Hurricane Center had never seen anything like this in the history of tracking storms. Zulu, a monster of a hurricane had disappeared off the radar system like a vapor.

BULLETIN 1 PM EST WED OCT 28 2020
POWERFUL CATEGORY FIVE HURRICANE
ZULU. . . HAS DISAPPEARED

30 SLEEPING BEAUTY

John approached Sister Abby with sadness in his heart. She saved his life, caring for him every day for twenty years. Now, the time had come for John to leave the island of Boatan, the mission, and his newly found family. "Sister... I think my heart is breaking."

"Mine too John! Please stay safe... *and remember me.*" Abby started to cry. "I stared at your sweet face for most of my adult life. I bathed you, fed you, and now I must say goodbye, it's so darn hard."

"You and the Padre are so special to me. I will never forget you Sister Abby," he reached out, embraced her, and wiped a tear from her cheek, "Please take care of the Padre, he is not as young as he thinks."

"John, the world is much different than when you fell asleep. It's a dark place now... even in America. PLEASE be careful. They will try to bio-tag you, and they may want to detain you, when you get home. Don't let them tag you!"

"I will Sister. I won't let them bio-tag me." John hugged her one more time, turned and walked over to the Padre's truck.

Cindy and Carl Moss sat on the majestic forward deck of their 204' twin diesel mega-yacht waiting for a visitor. Carl was a tech giant who turned a $10,000 loan into a multibillion-dollar company. Now retired, they cruise the Mediterranean and Caribbean... and currently are docked on the east end of the island of Boatan. They didn't know who was coming or why he'd be there.

The night before, Cindy awoke from a dream. She called out to her husband Carl, who, moments earlier also woke from a dream.

Carl rushed to the side of the bed and said, "Honey, are you okay?"

"Yes Carl, I had the most astonishing dream."

"You too...."

"Yes." She tried to lift herself up. Cindy is paraplegic as a result of a car accident she'd been in as a teen.

"Let me help you dear," Carl reached behind Cindy to adjust her pillows, "Tell me yours... and I'll tell you mine...."

Cindy reached up and brushed her short auburn hair away from her eyes with the palm of her hand. "I was wrapped in the wings of a beautiful blue and white angel. I saw myself standing.... You know, I always stand or walk in my dreams. I stood enveloped in a blue and white light. I've never felt so much comfort. The angel embraced me. A surge of peace rushed through my body. He lifted my chin. My eyes met the brilliant blue eyes of this amazing creature. He said, *'Cindy, my name is Raphael. I am an angel of the Most High God. You, dear sister, are greatly loved in heaven.'* He told me; tomorrow a man, by the name of John, was going to meet us on the dock. He said to invite him aboard and take him to Tampa.... He also said he had a gift for us."

"Astonishing! How can two people have the same dream?" Carl tried to wrap his logical mind around it. "I dreamt I saw you wrapped in the wings of an angel. An incredible blue and white light surrounded you as if the sky of heaven was over you. A voice said, *'Do what Cindy requests.'* I woke up, went outside, and stared at the night sky."

"Carl, we need to help this man."

"I understand dear, we will."

Now, morning had come. Cindy and Carl sat waiting....

The battered red truck stopped in front of the dock. John got out and walked over to the Padre. Too choked up to speak, he gave him a long, warm embrace... turned and made his way to the yacht.

The Padre yelled out, "Be careful son! Don't forget about us islanders... God's speed!" As John walked away, the despondent Padre thought, "*I wonder if I'll ever see him again?*

John reached the deep-water slip of Sleeping Beauty and approached the deckhand next to the ramp, "My name is John."

The deckhand yelled to the upper deck, "Ma'am, he's here." He turned to John, "Mr. and Mrs. Moss are expecting you sir. Please follow me."

John followed, as the deck hand pointed out the direction to his stateroom and various features of the ship, "Your stateroom is on the second level sir. Mr. and Mrs. Moss are on the first."

They walked around to the bow and were greeted by the Captain, "Good day sir, please follow me, I will take you to Mr. and Mrs. Moss."

John, amazed by the size and beauty of the boat, thought, "*Raphael sure knows how to make travel arrangements.*" They turned the corner... on a sofa, adjacent to the hot tub, sat Cindy and Carl Moss.

Carl stood up and walked over. "You must be John?" he said with a warm and hearty greeting.

"Yes sir, I am. Thank you so much for your hospitality."

"Come John; let me introduce you to my wife Cindy."

Cindy sat on the sofa with an afghan over her legs. Next to her was a wheelchair. "Oh my, you are so very real. Please sit. Let's get acquainted.... Our chef has prepared a wonderful meal for us."

"Why thank you. I'm grateful to be here!" Her kind face mesmerized John.

Carl said, "John, we should be on our way by 1300 hours. I hope you don't mind an early lunch?"

"Not at all sir."

During lunch, Cindy and Carl told John about their dreams. John told them about his amazing journey to Boatan, Padre Ramos, and Sister Abby. Carl said, "You know John, we believe in God and always give to the church, or at least we did... but after the war things changed... and we were left feeling hopeless. We left the mainland in 18, after the holocaust, and lived in the Bahamas for a bit, in search of a fresh start."

John smiled, "Mrs. Moss, I was wondering about your condition."

"Oh," Cindy said, "I was in a car accident when I was young. I'm paralyzed from the waist down." she sat in her wheelchair with her legs covered.

John said, "I'm sorry Mrs. Moss." Seconds later he sensed the prompting of the Holy Spirit, "Before we depart, if you don't mind, I would like to pray for you?"

Carl said, "You know John, we believe in God, and always give to the church, or at least we did, before the war. We left the mainland in 18, after the holocaust and lived in the Bahamas for a bit."

Feeling optimistic for the first time in years, Cindy said, "Please pray John, I would like that."

John turned towards Cindy, "Do you mind if I place my hand on your knee?"

"That would be fine."

John looked into Cindy's warm eyes and said, "The Father has a gift for you today."

"Yes, what is it?" she said trembling.

"Papa, show Cindy how much you love her...."

As he spoke, a mist from heaven fell, covering Cindy with God's presence. Dewdrops formed on her forehead and face, as droplets ran down her arms and hands.

John continued, "Healing rain Papa, bring your healing rain...."

The sky behind them thundered. Cindy closed her eyes, and then opened them, and looked up, "It's raining!" Her face became wet with the water of heaven. As she sat there crying, her legs started to spasm violently. "What's happening to me? God..."

"I release healing, in the name of our King," said John.

Carl stood behind Cindy gripping her shoulder, "John, what is happening to my wife?"

"Carl, it's okay, the father is bringing life to her legs. In Him is life, and His life is wrapped in tender love and grace."

A warm surge of energy ran up and down Cindy's legs and back. She cried out, "My legs are burning."

Carl asked, "You can feel your legs?" He started to cry.

As the energy increased, Cindy's legs shot straight out, shaking for several seconds... then slowly began to relax. John told Carl to remove her blanket. John took hold of her hands and said, "Come on Cindy, let's put your legs to work," then he gently helped her to her feet.

She trembled as she cried, "I can walk! Honey, I can walk!"

Raphael stood smiling at the amazing grace of the King.

31 SIDE TRIP

Nathan and his angelic team of warriors stood on the cement ramp at birth 5 in the Port of Manatee waiting for John's arrival. "Today, my warriors, we enter into a new chapter in this mission. Raphael and John will be here soon. We must keep our cover until John is safe in Pelican Bay."

"Understood Nathan," said Cayla.

"Cayla, go and prepare the driver for our journey."

"I found a good man for this mission," said Cayla. He took to the sky, headed for Ruskin.

Drones departed from a U.S. Coast Guard cutter and circled the waterways west of the port of Tampa. The Captain of Sleeping Beauty maintained course, moving away from Tampa, towards the port of Manatee. The Port Authority directed Sleeping Beauty into birth 5 where it was going to be transported to a dry-dock station for maintenance. Carl and Cindy said goodbye to John as he deboarded the ship, "John, here's my private line, reach out to me if you need anything, please, I'm a phone call away."

"Thank you Carl. You're a gracious man."

Cindy, overcome with emotion, said, "John, I'm speechless... **I can walk again!** You're a blessing." She was smiling on the outside, but inside... she wanted him to stay, "I'm so glad we could help you John. I wish you could stay with us for a while. Well be in Tampa."

"Cindy, I'm sorry I can't come with you guys. I need to get to my mother. Pelican Bay beckons me...."

"John, how are you going to get by Port Authority? Homeland Security and the Guardian Inspection station are at the end of the birth."

"I don't know Carl; I suppose I'll walk right through." He turned and walked down the ramp.

Cayla arrived in the back of a cargo delivery van. The driver ate lunch and started getting ready to depart towards Palmetto. Cayla was invisible.

John approached the double glass doors at the entrance of the PA Office. Unbeknownst to him, Nathan and four other angels led the way.

The entrance doors of the Port Authority flew open. A Guardian stationed near by, stepped outside to shut them. John walked towards the bio-tag pre-entry inspection point. Surprised that no one noticed his presence, he mumbled, "I guess this is going to be easier than I thought." He walked right past the officers and out the front door. The angels had blinded their eyes from seeing John. No one looked up. No one saw him coming.

Nathan said to Raphael, "I'm so glad you're back my friend. How are you? How is John? Is he ready for this journey?"

"I'm well Nathan... sweet move back there," said Raphael smiling. "John is strong. He is ready, the Padre's peace is upon him."

John made his way through the parking area down Terminal Street and walked towards Piney Point Rd. He turned left, walked 2.5 miles down County Line Road and came out at S. Tamiami Trail. When he got to the street, he stuck out his thumb for a ride.

As the cargo van's driver approached County Line Road, Cayla whispered into the driver's ear, "Pull over and give this man a ride."

The driver spotted John hitchhiking and pushed on his brakes. He pulled off the road and lowered his window, "Need a lift buddy?"

"You bet," said John, "Heading to Pelican Bay."

"Well get in, I'll take you."

John jumped into the van and placed his backpack behind the seat, "Thank you so much! My name is John."

"Glad to meet you John, my name is Barry."

Nathan and Cayla were in the back of the van. On the roof of the van sat sixteen warrior angels, their hands clutching swords of light.

As soon as they pulled out the Holy Spirit spoke to John, "Danny and Bryan were arrested. They're being held at the Rehabilitation Center in the old Manatee County Central Jail.... John, I am sending you, to set them free."

John thought, *"How am I going to do that?"*

The Lord spoke again, "Not by might, nor by power, but by My Spirit... shall you set them free."

As Barry turned the corner towards the Jail, John said, "Barry, please stop the van."

Cayla whispered into Barry's spirit, "*It's okay. Stop and wait.*"

"Ok John, not a problem. How long are you going to be?"

"Not long Barry. Thank you for waiting."

The Detention Center was thick with the presence of the demonic. John made his way up the sidewalk towards the entrance of the jail. Invisible angelic warriors flanked John. He opened the door to the lobby and walked in. Everyone in the building stared at him.

The Guardian on his left raised his weapon; growling in a demonic tone said, "Freeze!"

John turned to his left and raised his hand.

The Guardian flew backwards, sliding into the water fountain on the wall. Nathan and his team rushed the sides of the lobby. All the Guardians froze. The demons inside them cried out to the angelic team, "What do we have to do with you, angels of the Most High God?"

"SILENCE!" John said. He spoke directly to the demonic stronghold.

A Guardian responded in a manic voice, "This place is restricted!"

John turned to him and said; "I'm here on assignment, not on my own authority, but the authority of the one who has sent me." He looked up to heaven and said, "Papa!" A mighty wind began to swirl in the lobby. Plants, papers, chairs, and magazines flew in all directions. "*Peace*," said John. Instantly, heaven's mist began to fall. As the water vapors engulfed the Guardians, demons flew out of them screeching in torment. Nathan and his team subdued them. All the Guardians tumbled to the ground, lifeless, and in a deep sleep.

Danny and Bryon were held in the Rehabilitation Zone, on cellblock 23. The mist moved down the hallways overpowering all who crossed its path. As it reached cellblock 23, all the cells filled with mist... and the doors flung opened. John followed the cloud of mist and glanced down the hall. Danny and Bryon walked slowly out of their cells.

Bryon peered down the hall, transfixed by the strange mist, "John, is that you John?" He started to cry, "I can't believe it's you!" He ran towards John.

Danny saw Bryon running. His eyes met his, "John, is that you?" He limped after him.

John didn't wait. He dashed over and embraced Bryon.

"John, I thought you were dead. What is happening?" said Bryon.

"I'm alive as can be. We have to go, we're taking everyone with us." John said to a crowd of about 16 prisoners, "Friends, come with me, now. You're free." Then he took Danny's hand, "I'm so glad I found you Danny.... We need to go."

32 CITY OF LIGHT

Barry was surprised when John returned to the van with sixteen citizens walking behind him. He got out of the van to help the injured, "John, is this going to be a problem?"

"It's fine Barry. Don't be afraid. Everything is fine."

Cayla reached out and touched Barry on the head releasing peace into his spirit.

While they loaded the van, the boy, James McEnroe, called out to John, "Hey mister, thank you so much! What you did back there... I never... I mean who would believe it. Amazing!" He turned and walked towards the edge of the road.

John replied, "Aren't you coming with us?"

"I wish I could," replied the boy, "I need to find my parents.... Hey mister, what's your name?"

"My name is John."

"My mane is James.... Thank you John, I will never forget this day!"

"You're welcome James. Be safe out there."

The van approached Mangrove Avenue. Bryon's head rested on John's shoulder. Danny said, "I can't believe my eyes Johnny, you're almost home."

"How is my mother?"

"She's amazing John. Your mother always believed you were alive, and would come home to her."

"And Phil?"

"Still strong as an ox, but he's old now John," said Danny. "He left the Sheriff's office after the war started."

"Why, it was his life?"

"Everything changed John. Nothing's the same anymore...."

Bryon spoke up, "Barry, turn left at the stop sign. It's the last house on the right. You can park on the side, behind that rusty bus."

"My bus, I can't believe they kept it," said John, as the van pulled up and turned off the headlights.

Sara heard the van pull up. She peeked out of the window to see who it was. "Nikita, there's a group of people behind the house," then she recognized Danny and Bryon, "Hurry Nikita, Danny is home!"

Nikita rushed downstairs and opened the door. Her eyes met Danny's, "Oh my God...." She ran to him and leaped into his arms. He hugged her tightly. "How did you get out?"

He turned. Standing next to him was John, "Nikita, look who's home."

John reached out and touched her hair with is hand, "Hi Niki," he paused, "Where's my mother?" Nikita's eyes teared up. She embraced him, and then turned her head towards the front door.

John glanced in that direction. Standing in the doorway was a silver-haired woman dressed in a light blue sweater. "Mom? Is that you?" He wedged his way through the crowed and ran to the porch, "Mom... it's me, Johnny. I'm home!" He reached out and picked her up off her feet hugging her tightly.

Sara started crying, "Johnny, I knew you would come home to me! I knew you were alive." Sara was overjoyed.

She waited so long, "Honey, help me inside, I need to sit down." She was 78 years old, strong, but overwhelmed.

John and Sara sat in the living room. Nikita helped everyone inside taking them upstairs to the upper room, now converted to a sanctuary for runaway citizens. Nikita and Danny moved in with Phil and Sara when the persecution started.

A short while later, Phil walked through the door. "Honey, there's a brown cargo van parked...." He stopped mid-sentence. His eyes met John's.

"Dad, it's me. I'm home."

Phil dropped his hat and cane, "John? Oh my, I can't believe it! Is that really you?"

John stood up and walked over to him, "Here dad, let me help you." Phil was 80, and had trouble walking.

That night they all sat out back, next to the fire pit, and listened to John as he shared his adventure with everyone. The crowd was astonished.... They, in turn, brought John up to speed on all that had transpired while he was away.

Pastor Ron removed the boards nailed across the front doors of the church. He walked back, switched on the breakers, and turned on the lights. He didn't care if the authorities found out. Hope was in the air.

Three hours later the church bells rang out across the town of Pelican Bay. A large crowd formed outside the chapel. Inside, it was full to capacity. Everyone heard about John's return. Pastor Ron asked John if he would address the town.

Pastor Ron opened prayer and introduced Sara. She glanced over at John, smiled, and slowly walked to the microphone, "Good afternoon my friends and family," she paused looking around at the crowd, "I haven't seen this many people gather in our town for a long time. Surly, it's not for a little old lady," she said smiling. The crowd laughed and let out a loud applause. "I always believed my Johnny was alive. I always believed he would come home to our town. I want to thank you for coming out today. Do you mind if my Johnny speaks to you today?"

The crowd responded with enthusiastic "Yeses" and "whistles."

"Let me introduce you to my son, John Parker."

John stood and walked to the front of the stage, embraced his mother and took the microphone, "Thank you all for being here today and giving me such a warm welcome. 21 years ago Bryon and I pushed off Higgins Marina in Methuselah II, bound for Belize." He glanced over at Bryon and motioned for him to stand. Bryon stood and nodded, then quickly sat back down, "We made our way down the coast, stopping in Key West for supplies before we sailed on to the Dry Tortugas. Days later, we rounded our way past Cuba. The weather was clear and the night sky sparkled with a blanket of stars.... A massive storm came out of nowhere. Our boat was hammered from end to end. We were hit by a monstrous rogue wave and rolled repeatedly. Our mast broke and started pulling us in to the deep. We were sure we were going to sink and drown.... Bryon was hit in the head and bled furiously. We were taking on water. We were in danger." John paused for a second and looked around. That silent pause had the audience at the edge of their seats.

"I told Bryon I was going back out to cut away the sail before we sank.... Bryon warned me not to go, but I did what I had to do. I wasn't harnessed. We were struck by two massive waves.... Sandwiched between two walls of water, I was knocked down and fell into the sea.... The currents were so powerful I couldn't get to the surface.... I started sinking.... I kept drifting down.... I could see, through the blue water, my boat rolling above me. I tried to hold my breath and swim, but I kept on sinking. I was face up.... The waters became dark. I could feel my life leaving me.... Then I felt a hand take hold of me, and I passed out." The emotions of remembering took hold of him.

"When I woke I was lying on the beach on the island of Boatan. I was only awake for a moment, but in that moment, my eyes met the eyes of an angel. He touched me, and said 'sleep.' The next thing I remember was opening my eyes and staring into the face of a nun. It was twenty years later.... Sister Abby and Padre Ramos took care of me for the last 20 years. Every day the sister rolled me over to avoid bedsores. She bathed me and fed me through a tube. Every night the Padre prayed over me and read to me from the scriptures. He made a cot next to mine and slept by my side for 20 years. We were at the Mision Santa Rosalia on the island of Boatan, outside Honduras...."

"...When I woke I had amnesia. I couldn't remember my name, who I was, or where I came from. For the next six months, Sister Abby worked with me, getting me to a place where I was strong enough to walk. It worked! I not only walked... but also ran... every day, on the beach, in front of the mission, trying to remember....

In October, a category 4 Hurricane, named Zulu, zeroed in on the island of Boatan. I stood in the shelter helping Sister Abby with the children. Their frightened faces hurt my heart. I ran out of the shelter and down to the beach. The wind and the rain was blowing at over 60 knots. That's when it happened.... That's when my memory came back....

I cried out to God.... My mind was filled with memories of my past. The Lord spoke to me, 'Why do you say, 'I'm just a boy'? I have given you a new identity. On this day, you shall be known as My Rain King. No longer will you say 'I am just a boy.' Today, you are a 'Son of Thunder.' Then He paused. His words penetrated deep into my spirit... Then He said, 'Today is the day! Today the power of this storm is in the palms of your hands. Now, speak to the storm and tell it to cease, SPEAK JOHN!' So I raised my arms and cried out to the storm, 'I command you Zulu... I command you in the name of the King, BE SILENT.... Waters BE calm!' Instantly, as if a massive hand covered the 160-mile wide hurricane and smothered it, 'POOF'... it was gone. A blanket of peace fell over the region." John's testimony captivated the crowd.

John continued, "Sometimes God, with incredible wisdom, power, and strength, will hide you in the palm of His hand.... Like an old pocket watch, He pulls you out of your hiding place.... *because it's time....*" He paused, gazing at the crowd, "I know that all of you have been through horrible things, the last several years. I know many of you are fearful. Some have lost loved ones. Others have had friends or family, turn on you, or abandon you. Many today believe that rebellion, and taking up arms, is the answer to deal with the darkness at hand. Others cower in fear, hiding, and waiting for the rapture.

We must understand, the power, peace, and love, the Son of God gave to His bride, the church. We must understand that our God is a good God, all the time. His grace endures forever. It is only by His hand that light overcomes darkness.

I am here to tell you today, that this is the day of salvation. Now is the time for revealing the sons and daughters of God. Today you will see the glory of our King and know the hope that lies within you. You my friends will be a city set on a hill. Your light will shine brightly, in this dark world. Your borders will be expanded. No longer shall you fear, form out from this town a light will shine forth and this city shall be a city of refuge. Even now, many of you are feeling the power of the Holy Spirit upon you. At the sound of my voice the Father is demonstrating His love towards you."

Many in the audience began to cry. Their hearts opened up to heaven's gift. John said, "Now I am going to pray for you... please just sit back and receive what Jesus is giving you this day." Then he prayed, "Papa, I ask you by your sweet and tender mercy, rain down upon us your love Papa. Rain down and bring about a city of light. Touch your children and fill them with your glory Papa, that they might know they are the extension of your hand."

As John prayed, a mighty mist filled the sanctuary. A thick cloud infused with Holy water covered the people. As the mist touched them they started to cry. They were filled with the joy of His presence. The Spirit of God fell on the church. Many stood to their feet with hands lifted to heaven, soaking wet, and praising the King of Heaven and Earth. Others lay prostrate, their face to the ground, sobbing. Many saw angels surrounding them. Others said they saw a canopy of light over the church.

Sara sat weeping and praising God with lifted hands, as her face was covered with heaven's dew. She remembered her vision, 40 years earlier... before John was born, how she flew in the midst of the rain on the wings of a dove. That same day she received the promise of his birth. She took hold of Phil's hand and squeezed it, "I love you Phil."

It started raining outside. Unaware of what was transpiring at the church, and for reasons unexplained, people flooded the streets—drawn by the rain. As the rain fell upon them, their eyes were opened to the majesty of God's glory. People cried out to God for salvation. With tenderness and mercy, He touched each and every one of them. The healing mist moved over the sick and they recovered. The blind, lame, and weak were touched by the love of God. The Latter Rain had come to Pelican Bay!

Nathan gathered his team outside the church and said, "Raphael, this city is now a city for our King. Dispatch the Holy Guardians, establish the boarder, and place shields of light at every corner. Today we have the first City of Refuge. There are many, many more to come."

"Yes Nathan, today is a glorious day."

"Team, I am being summoned to the council of the King. Peace to you my brothers. The King is with you."

"Also with you my friend, also with you." They said in one accord.

Then Nathan turned and flew up through the heavens, his hair wet with the presence of God.

EPILOGUE

I will never forget the day when John walked through the mist at Manatee Jail. It changed my heart and soul forever. The next time I met John was in Lone Tree Colorado, in the summer of 25.

I walked into the church of the redeemer, surrounded by crowds, as the mist of heaven fell on them. Thousands came to Christ. I stood in the back of the church. Next to me, a veteran of the war, sat in a wheelchair. Half his face disfigured. With a bowed head, he cried. The mist of heaven fell on him and his face restored to perfect condition. Overwhelmed by the miracle, the veteran began to shake. He pushed aside his wheelchair and stood to his feet crying and praising God. Later, I asked him what happened. He simply said, "I was blind, but now I see.... I was lame but now I stand...."

Afterwards, I approached John, "I'm not sure if you remember me? James, my name is James."

"James, didn't we meet at the Manatee Jail?"

"Yes, it changed my life. Do you mind if I interview you for The Remnant."

"I would love that James, I've read your work. Your gift is a blessing to the body of Christ."

We talked for some time. I asked about his mission. I asked where we all were headed. "John, Chancellor Damian's power stretches around the globe. What should we, the faithful, do?"

He stared at me, and then said, "James, it is critical for the faithful to seek the presence and power of our King. It is so important. His presence brings the light. By His power, love, and mercy, hearts are changed... cities are transformed. We are the sons of light. There is a sleeping giant inside each of us... waiting to be set free. Dwelling in the presence of Christ releases the giant within! There is only one mission James: to bring the kingdom of our King to earth.... Tell them not to focus on darkness, rather focus on the light. Jesus is the Light of the World."

John paused for a second, "All around the world—it's going to rain down, everywhere you turn—it's going to rain down. It is time for the Latter Rain, James."

"John, there are rumors that many 'Sons of Thunder,' like yourself, are scattered around the world. Can you comment on those rumors?"

"Yes James, there are. A son of thunder is bringing the power and message of the King, to every region. The important thing to remember—we all are children of light. God is calling the nations into His presence. Tell your readers to bring the Kingdom, to bring heaven's rain and light to the world. We all are meant to be, Sons and Daughters of Thunder!"

"What is your destiny?"

"Destiny is waiting for everyone. The key is to find yours and fulfill the call of the Creator on your life.... Destiny is at the tip of your fingers.... Embrace His kingdom call and bring heaven to earth!" Then he paused, and reached for his bible and began to read from Revelation 10:

> "I saw still another mighty angel coming down from heaven, clothed with a cloud. And a rainbow was on his head, his face was like the sun, and his feet like pillars of fire. He had a little book open in his hand. And he set his right foot on the sea and his left foot on the land, and cried with a loud voice, as when a lion roars. When he cried

out, seven thunders uttered their voices. Now when the seven thunders uttered their voices, I was about to write; but I heard a voice from heaven saying to me, "Seal up the things which the seven thunders uttered, and do not write them.

The angel whom I saw standing on the sea and on the land raised up his hand to heaven and swore by Him who lives forever and ever, who created heaven and the things that are in it, the earth and the things that are in it, and the sea and the things that are in it, that there should be delay no longer, but in the days of the sounding of the seventh angel, when he is about to sound, the mystery of God would be finished, as He declared to His servants the prophets"

John closed the book and said, "The days of the Seven Thunders are here. Prepare for the coming of our King."

Many incredible things have happened since John's return. I'm sure this wave of grace is happening throughout the world, and I expect many more waves to come in the near future, as the kingdom of God fills the planet with His glory!

One final thought for you, the remnant of the King— seek His face, and know... the King is with you! Prepare for, and release, the rain.

James McEnroe,

a faithful servant of the King

ABOUT THE AUTHOR

Fred Raynaud is author of seven books, a speaker, coach, Chef by trade, and servant of the King. He lives on the Island of Anna Maria with his wife Jan.

"And it shall come to pass in the last days, says God,
That I will pour out of My Spirit on all flesh;
Your sons and your daughters shall prophesy,
Your young men shall see visions,
Your old men shall dream dreams" - Acts 2:17

The
Seer's
Gift

A Look at the Language of Visions & Dreams

God's incredible gifting in the life of a believer

FRED L. RAYNAUD

"And when Jesus went out He saw a great multitude;
and He was moved with compassion for them, and
healed their sick"
- Mark 14:14

The
Seer
&
Healing

The Seer Gift and the
Ministry of Healing

FRED L. RAYNAUD

The
Seer
&
Prophecy

The Gift and Office of the Seer Prophet

FRED L. RAYNAUD

"I have also spoken by the prophets, and I have multiplied visions, and used similitudes, by the ministry of the prophets"
- Hosea 12:10, KJV

The
Seer's
Guide to
Symbolism

Similitudes, Metaphors, & Symbolism

FRED L. RAYNAUD

Made in the USA
Middletown, DE
24 April 2016